Patsy (Cline) Stewart's

Little Black Box

Copyright ©

2012 E.M.Shannon

A special thank you to Simon, and my daughters for all their support and encouragement.

To my best pal Linda for believing in me.

And a BIG! Thank you, to Carol and Sharon my nieces, for all their hard work proof reading my novel, and also helping with the publishing of my book.

CHAPTER 1

Losing My Dream

It was a cold winter's night in November 1967. I was all tucked up in bed looking out the window from the top flat of our tenement building. Tears streaming down my face. It was now the early hours of the morning, but I couldn't sleep. I was still in shock; I was repeatedly churning over the explanations in my head. But STILL! I couldn't understand WHY? OH! WHY! Are they against me?

Mum and dad, who for reasons I am unable to comprehend, were not in favour of me going to university. But WHY couldn't I go?

Recently it has become a constant argument in our house, with me trying desperately to make my parents listen to what I wanted out of life. But the outcome has always the same ending with the three of us screaming, obnoxious remarks at each other. These fights have taken their toll, and left me feeling very sad, and deeply depressed.

I just want to DIE…

I had my wet face pressed up tight against the windowpane, and the freezing glass as it hit my cheek didn't even produce a tiny flicker of life, in my now unoccupied body. Nothing was penetrating my soul, and forcing me back to reality. I was in an empty place.

My eyes without thinking were automatically studying the dark empty street below; hoping somehow for a miracle, but knowing deep down that nothing, was ever going to alter their decision.

My brain, despite my low mood could faintly register the familiar sound of " Stand By Me " playing softly in the background; but I was unable to stop the uncontrolled tears falling down my cheeks. I blankly stared out of the window, desperately trying to come to terms with losing my dream.

When suddenly! Outside, there was a flurry of snow, and the red glow from the old gas lamps, was bouncing off the snow, creating a pink shimmer of light as it fell onto the ground. It was like someone had sprinkled pink fairy dust, but it was only there for a second, and then the magic was gone...

Everything in life changes; but at fifteen the prospect of change can be very daunting. To be expected to go to school one day, and then the next to have a full time job was to me unrealistic.

I was only a daft wee lassie from the south side of Glasgow. Just turned fifteen, and expected to leave school at Christmas. I knew I wasn't ready, But no one was listening. I was still playing kick the can, FOR GODSAKE!

I have persistently tried my utmost to convince my mum and dad that I had the ability to study, and that one day I could become a teacher. But it was a completely hopeless exercise ending up with the three of us, all shouting at each other at the same time in a heated debate. It was just pandemonium!

" Ma why can ah no stay on at school, and become a teacher or sumthing? " I pleaded.

" Whit, Patsy, are ye aff yer heed? Wasting four years o' yer life when ye can be oot earning some money before ye leave the hoose, and get merried, " was her hasty reply.

" But ma, not everywan wants to get merried and hev kids, " I pleaded.

Mum gave me one of her deadliest looks, and her twisted expression conveyed her obvious annoyance. I turned, and focussed my anger towards my dad.

" Da, Da, hev ye no got onything tae say! " I yelled.

" Yer maw's right, nae use in wasting time educating ye. Then ye aboot turn, and get merried! " He shouted as he left the room banging the door behind him.

" BUT! But ma, can ye no let me at least TRY? " I said, letting out a big weary sigh.

" Na! Na! Yer faither and I hev discussed it and yer leaving, " she bawled back at me.

GREAT! I might as well throw in the towel, because it is an utter waste of time trying to battle out anything with mum. When she's made up her mind, nothing I could say would change it. There was no point going over, and over the argument. My feelings were not important, and I would just have to learn to accept my fate. Mum was mapping out my destiny with no consideration about how I felt.

BUT! Who gave, HER the right to make that decision?

My MUM: by the way left school at fourteen. Married at sixteen. She had four kids, three boys, and a girl. I was the baby of the family. If she had been happily married then MAYBE! I could have understood her theory, wanting the same happiness for her only daughter, but her life wasn't a bed of roses.

No far from it! Mum was constantly fighting with dad, and there were some awful days of full-scale aggression between them, when all the ornaments were physically thrown at each other. Then the following day there would be a very slight ceasefire, but they would still repeatedly bicker away at each other until the next battle began. There never seemed be a truce only a pause to reload their guns.

Mum should have sought greater expectations for her baby girl!!!

CHAPTER 2

Mr and Mrs Stewart

Mum was over forty when she had me, but not many women had babies at her age in the 1950's. It was considered to be far too old, and I'm sure the stigma of having a late baby, when your youngest son was twenty, wasn't good. She would have been the talk of the STEAMIE (A place where everyone goes to do they're washing). I don't think she ever forgave me.

" Hey did ye hear aboot Mrs Stewart she's haying anither wain, " said the first woman standing at the sink washing her clothes.

" Whit's she been up tae ah wonder at her age, " second woman said grinning.

" Your jist jealous cause your Billy's past it, " then the whole line of women who were ear wigging to the juicy gossip all squealed with laughter.

" You must be joking hev ye seen hur man? " The steamie was in an uproar with everyone throwing in their tuppence worth.

Mum is only five feet tall, big busted with hips to match. She is like a wee barrel, and I'm certain that if she fell over, and was shoved in the right direction, she would roll quite easily. She might be small, but she has very strong arms, and hands like shovels. She really is a sturdy looking wee wuman.

But her tongue is her most powerful secret weapon she could cut you up, and spit you out before you could say

" Bob's yer uncle. " Her reputation is well known in oor neighbourhood; no one would ever give her any grief except, that is, my dad.

Mum has dyed brown hair that she has set in the same style every week. Short curls that looked like the rollers were left behind. Her hair never moves because it is cemented with lacquer. It stays exactly the same until she goes back to the hairdresser the following week.

If it rains, which is a regular occurrence in Glasgow, she would wear a clever wee contraption called a rain mate, which is a plastic scarf type thing that she keeps in her handbag, for any unexpected emergencies. Only adults wore these foreign garments, us teenagers wouldn't be seen dead in them regardless of how bad the weather was.

Mum's eyes are dark brown, but they never look happy. Sometimes I wondered if I was the reason mum appeared to be so miserable? All the boys had left the house, and for the first time in her married life, she could have had time to herself.

My late arrival must have been a shock to her, and caused havoc to mum's now quiet household. (That is to say only quiet when dad was at the pub) OR! She could have been delighted, and relished in the experience of having her first baby girl, and spoiled her rotten.

But NO! Such LUCK!

Dad on the other hand, is a wee wiry man not much bigger than mum. He looks a lot older than his sixty years. (Too many whisky's, and Woodbine cigarettes I think). He's been completely bald from an early age, with Eric Morecambe glasses, and greeny blue eyes. Just like mine. But his, dress sense is stuck in the 1920's. He is still wearing twenty-two inch wide trouser legs, the type that you only see clowns wearing, and Pa Broon braces to hold them up. He also has silver coloured elastic type bands to stop his sleeves falling down, but the classic is his granddad shirt. It has a separate collar, which is attached with tiny studs. These studs, and collars were forever getting lost, and were the cause of many a major upset in our wee flat on a number of occasions. When this happens his face turns scarlet, his eyes look like they're about to pop out of their sockets, and he does a wee dance stamping his feet up and down the lobby. He's like a two year old having a tantrum. There were times when I was convinced he was about to burst a major blood vessel. Why could he no just wear a normal SHIRT?

Dad; nevertheless was very clever at school, which I find hard to believe. He even managed to become the school dux, but tragically his dad died in the First World War, leaving his mother (my granny Stewart) a widow. She then had to raise her four children on her own. Dad, being the eldest, was given no choice but to leave school at the age of fourteen, and find a job to help support his mother. Something he has always regretted. He still, however, was able to become an engineer, and has a good secure job, but it never seemed to be enough.

He is, I'm sorry to say a very selfish man. Spending all his free time in the pub drinking as much alcohol that his wee body could possibly consume without falling down, but on most occasions he miscalculates the amount, and ends up staggering all over the place. Once he broke his nose falling onto the pavement, but insisted that he had slipped on some slimy mysterious substance that someone had accidentally dropped onto the ground.

Alcohol always puts a big smile on his face, but his smile always fades very rapidly when the booze has disappeared out of his system. He then reverts back to crabbie old Mr. John Stewart.

Not being able to go to university, and always regretting not having been given the chance to learn, I thought dad would have encouraged me to make a career for myself. But unfortunately, he is too wrapped up in his own importance to become involved in my future. I truly believe he is jealous of the opportunity I could have.

My brothers were given more scope. They were all encouraged to go to university, or learn a trade. All three of them decided on a trade.

But because I'm just a mere girl I don't have a CHOICE!

CHAPTER 3

Old Black And White Movies

Mum's biggest weakness is watching movies. She loves anything to do with glamour, and celebrities. And for that reason she proceeded to christened all her children with names of famous Hollywood stars. Although dad objected strongly, his words fell on deaf ears.

" Are ye crazy wuman; nae bodie in Scotland calls ther son Kirk Douglas!! I'll be a laughing stock. "

Secretly I think mum deliberately wanted to annoy dad, and she took great pleasure in getting her own way.
My granny Stewart told me many times about how my mum harped on and on wearing my dad down. Threatening to stop cooking his meals, and leaving him to look after the new baby. Dad reluctantly had to give in; looking after a baby was not an option, how would he get his alcohol fix?

Kirk Douglas Stewart is my oldest brother at thirty-nine. He is the tallest standing five feet ten; with dark brown hair, and brown eyes. Kirk is a handsome man, and he is very fortunate to have inherited my granny Stewart's warm smile.

Although he had the film star good looks, Kirk had no acting ability, which was to be a big disappointment to mum, who I'm sure was hoping Kirk, would have some talent, and that someday he would fulfil her dreams, and whisk mum off to Hollywood to live next to her favourite celebrities. But he had no interest in the movies, and quite happily became an electrician instead.

Kirk is lucky; he earns a good living from his job. But he was married before I was born, making a bond between us very difficult. Kirk also has two boys, and lives at the west end of Glasgow. They don't visit very often, which is a shame, because it would be good to have more contact with my nephews.

Paul is Kirks eldest son. He's going to be tall like his dad; he's five feet eight already, and he's only just turned fourteen. Michael is the baby at twelve years old, and he is the spitting image of his mother with auburn hair, blue eyes, and with a massive amount of freckles covering the whole of his face.

Kirk's wife Helen is a lovely woman, but with an over friendly personality. She can wear you down; she never stops talking. She has the most annoying technique where she can quite easily expand simple conversation, and drag it out for hours, and hours.

" Cauld the day Patsy, and whit aboot that rain yisterday, well I wis caught oot we nae brolly, and a pair o' open sandals ma feet were soaking, blab...blab...blab... " Helen goes on, and on without stopping for a breath of air.

" Aye, aye ah know, " I said in between her ranting.

Kirk, and his family only visit for special events (Birthdays, Christmas) when I assume he can't say no to mum, but they never stay long. I can still remember on numerous occasions when I was a wee lassie, Kirk lecturing dad on his drinking habits, and then the two of them would end up almost at each other throats. Kirk's biggest gripe was that dad should cut down on his drinking, and start treating mum with some respect. But dad couldn't see any harm in his alcohol consumption, or his behaviour towards mum.

" Da, can ye no go easy on the booze, and spend a wee bit mair time we maw? "

" Dinnae tell me wit tae dae, ah only hae a couple o' drams, " dad insisted.

" Are ye sure aboot that? "

" Ah'm oot o' here. Ye've got nae respect fir yer faither ."

Furious, dad would put his coat on. BANGING! The front door as he left the house.
I've a sneaky feeling; Kirk is mum's favourite son, because when he visits, she actually looks happy, and no matter what the topic she always agrees with Kirk.
Mum was a big Dean Martin fanatic; so needless to say she called her second son Dean Martin Stewart. What a shame he didn't have Dean's good looks, or was able to sing, but unfortunately he wasn't blessed with either. Instead he inherited all of dad's bad features, his small

frame, his poor eyesight, and of course dad's distinctive bald head.

Although, I have to say Dean's dress sense is far more superior than dad's clown outfit. Not being able to sing didn't deter Dean's future; he became a successful builder to trade, and then decided to open his own Company. He moved to England about ten years ago, and I am told he is a bit of a playboy with a string of beautiful girls running after him. But none of them have been able to get him hooked YET!

It must be his money that's the big attraction. It's definitely not his good looks. Needless to say I never see much of him either, making a brother and sister relationship non-existent.

Mum's youngest son was named Fred Astaire Stewart. Poor Fred, he also couldn't live up to his namesake, he was born with two left feet. But although he couldn't dance, he can sing, and play the guitar. Fred, really is quite a good singer, and can imitate Dean Martin's singing with an impressive Italian accent. What a shame, mum got it WRONG! She should have called Fred, Dean Martin.

Fred is the tiniest, just five foot two very slim like dad, but with an abundance of jet-black tight curly hair (A Jimmy Hendrix hair-do.) it's lucky for Fred his hair fits in well with the hippy trend of the era. Despite the obvious twenty-year age gap I still feel very close to him.

Fred became a joiner, but his first love is music. He was married at eighteen, but sadly it didn't work out. Fred's wife left him for another man, after only one year of marriage. I guess they were married far too young. Fred's now divorced, and always appears to be happy, and content with his life. He spends most of his free time singing, and playing the guitar. Sometimes my pal Linda, and I go and support him at his gigs.

Fred's hair, you can imagine is a bit of a joke in the family, except with dad. Dad is unable to get his head round the amount, and the type of hair Fred has. The comments start the minute Fred comes into the house. Dad immediately begins with the derogative remarks.

" Ah wisht ah knew where ye got aw that curly hair son, nae body in oor family ever hud ony tight curls, " dad would say in disgust.

Mum would get involved. " Whit ar ye trying tae say FAITHER?? " She was now losing control.

"I'm no saying onything. I'm only making an OBSERVATION, " dads voice getting louder.

"Aye, ah know, but ye make the same ALLEGATION every time ye see Fred, ah'm getting a bit tired o' aw yer insults," mum now out of her chair, and on her feet ready for a heated brawl.

" There's nae point talking tae ye, ah'm oot o' here. "

Dad was out the door before mum had a chance to get anywhere near him.
What a shame, poor Fred had hardly got time to put his bum on a seat before mum, and dad had caused a disturbance, giving dad an excellent excuse to go to the boozers.

I'm certain dad's real problem is he's seething with jealousy because he would love to have had HAIR! Of any DESCRIPTION!!

CHAPTER 4

Patsy

PATSY! That's ME! I was your typical teenager of the sixty's. I love the Beatles, Elvis, Tamla Motown, Everly Brothers, and Bob Dylan, OH! Aye, and don't forget Dean Martin; Doris Day; Paul Newman; to mention just a few.

Like mum, I also love all the old black and white movies; I would watch " It's A Wonderful Life " and " Casablanca " without fail every Christmas. And I still cried as if I had just seen it for the first time. But I'm sure there was a tiny bit of brainwashing going on while watching these films?

At fifteen it was easy to believe; you met a good-looking guy; you fell in love, and lived happily ever after. If only that was true!!!

However, I did suss out very quickly that you had to be really sure you picked the right one. Otherwise you were DOOMED! for the rest of your life. But, mum and dad obviously didn't make that connection.

I don't know why? They got married so young. But I did suspect that mum was pregnant which isn't the best of reasons. I was determined I wasn't going to let the same thing happen to me. Oh! No! I would be different. How naive can someone be!

I may not be the cherry on top of the fairy cake, but I do have some good qualities. I have long poker straight fair hair. Which is very fashionable at the moment. I am five foot three, not too small, but not too tall either. I am slim, but not as skinny as Twiggy. I'm sure my best feature is my eye's they are a lovely greeny-blue colour. Put it altogether, and it makes quite a good package.

When I was born mum's passion was still sitting in front of the telly watching old black and white movies with Fred Astaire, and Ginger Roger's films, being her favourite at the time, and so, she decided to name me Ginger Rodgers Stewart. Perhaps she wanted a partner for Fred?

BUT! THANK GOD! For granny, Stewart's intervention she managed to get mum to compromise, and call me after mum's beloved Patsy Cline instead.

But poor mum, I was unable to sing a note, after hours, and hours of wasted singing lessons from an old retired singing teacher who lived in our street. I was to become another statistic in my mother's plan of stardom. She had great aspirations for all her children, hoping that at least one of us would have been talented enough to one day snatch her away from her monotonous existence, and live a life of luxury in Hollywood. Fat CHANCE!

Although Patsy Cline wasn't that well known to my friends; I still never disclosed my middle name to anyone, except to my best pal Linda, whom I knew I could trust to keep my secret safe. But, could you imagine being called Ginger at school in GLASGOW! Of all places (Where ginger is another name for lemonade.)

" Hey, Ginger dae ye want some o' ma ginger? " I'm sure I would have been an easy target for jokes.

I have a lot of friends at school, but I am really; really, fortunate to have a pal like Linda. We only met three years ago, when she joined our class for the first year of secondary education. We clicked from the start, and now have a bond which I'm certain will last a lifetime.
Linda has a mass of beautiful long jet-black wavy hair, and big brown sexy eyes, that have a certain sparkle to them. She might only be five foot. But her personality is bigger than Scotland. She even makes my dad laugh when he's sober, which is unheard of.

" Still wearing those baggy troosers Mr. Stewart, hev ye no seen the new drain-pipe troosers yet? " Joked Linda.

" Aye, Linda, I'll be going up the toon next week tae hev a wee look, " dad laughed.

" Well ye better hurry up, cos there's a sale on in the boy's department in C&A's, " she teased.

" Is that so, well ah better no waste ony time, don't want tae miss a bargain, " dad said almost choking with laughter.

Dad can't help but laugh. Linda is such a funny character. If it were someone other than Linda he would be complaining that they had no manners, and he would have thrown them out the house for insulting him. Maybe I should try the jokes. NA! I don't think so. He would just do his normal moan. " That's no way to talk tae yer faither, " would be his stroppy reply.

I should have been the apple o' my dad's eye, being the only girl. But, that wasn't to be. He was never interested in anything I had to say. His philosophy in life is that children should be seen, and not heard. Anyway, who needed parents? I had Linda, and, there's always my precious record collection.

My big dream has now been shattered, and, although I wished with all my heart that things could be different. I had no power to stop the way my life was being launched, or the forces by which my destiny was being shaped. I knew I was going in the wrong direction. But what could I DO?

If only my granny Stewart was still alive she would have stood up for me. She would have had a good argument for my defence. Granny, I'm sure, would have told dad he was wrong to victimise me because I was a GIRL!!!

And, I know dad would have listened to his beloved mother. It's the only women he would never argue with, he loved, and respected her too much. Maybe, just maybe he would have been a better dad if granny Stewart were still alive.

My granny was known for her fairness, and she would have been incensed at what my parents were enforcing on her only grand daughter. She was a lovely old lady with the same greeny-blue eye's, and a warm smile that would make you feel welcome the minute she greeted you, and she always gave me a big hug every time we met.

Oh! How I miss HER...

CHAPTER 5

My First Job

Although reluctant to start work, I did manage to find a job very quickly as an office junior in an electrical firm's office. It was in the centre of Glasgow. Which meant that, I was up earlier, and out of the house for longer periods. I found the travelling in and out of town very tiring, and I struggled to adapt to the long hours of starting at eight, and finishing at five. I was always worn out, at the end of the day.

I felt I had fell into the deep end of the swimming pool, but didn't know how to swim. I didn't realise how much of a doddle school was, starting at nine o'clock, and finishing at four o'clock. Oh how, I wish I could go back.

The electrical repair shop is a father, and son's business. John Marshall was the father. He is a very handsome man; I think he's in his early fifties. He has a full head of dark hair with a touch of grey sprinkled above each ear. A small thin man who is always immaculately dressed in a black suit with a Persil white shirt. But best of all is his character. He is so easy to talk to, very kind, helpful, and encouraging. I couldn't help wishing my dad had a few of Mr. Marshall's fine qualities.

I would love to say the same about his son Gordon. Although he is blessed with his father's good looks, he was unfortunately right at the back of the queue when they were giving out personality. He has a definite small man syndrome.

Gordon is always looking for faults in my work, he's like a vulture waiting on his prey, ready to jump out at any opportunity, and chastise me. I was forever being shouted at in the house, but to be reprimanded in public in full view of all the office staff was humiliating, and embarrassing I was MORTIFIED!!!

I was already finding the transition from school to full time work very tough, and the last thing I needed was someone like Gordon making my life more difficult, by constantly picking faults. I wouldn't have minded if his criticism had been more constructive, but I'm sure he got a kick out of making me look silly in front of everyone.

Part of my job was to answer the phone, and it was taken for granted that I could carry out this task without any training. We didn't have a telephone at home. But, sometimes my mum phoned my aunty Joan, from a call box, and I was allowed to say HELLO! And, CHEERIO! Aunty Joan.

My limited experience was obvious to everyone, and it went from bad to worse. Every time the phone in the office rang I almost jumped out of my skin I just panicked. I got all my words mixed up. I knew I had to work on my pronunciation, and that my accent was far too strong. I needed HELP!!!.

This was all a new practice for me and I quickly recognized that I was way out of my depths. I knew trying to deal with this situation was going to be extremely difficult.

Mr. Marshall would be patient with me. He would call the office, and act out a scenario, pretending he was a customer looking for some information. I always knew it was Mr. Marshall. He had such a distinctive husky sounding voice, but I was grateful to him, for trying his best to help me sort out my predicament.

" Patsy, I called you today, you did really well. I couldn't have done any better myself, " he said encouragingly.

" Did you really Mr. Marshall I would never have know it was you, " I said trying to sound surprised when he exposed his true identity, and not wanting him to know I knew all along that it was him who had called me.

Gordon on the other hand would go to great lengths to inform me that some of his clients were complaining about the way I answered the phone. He never gave a thought for my feelings. Or to the fact that this was my first job, and I was only a fifteen-year-old girl currently left school. Why could he not just leave me alone?

After the first week I was a total wreck. Crying myself to sleep every night. Only Linda knew how upset I was. Without her reassurance I don't know how I could ever have got through another day. I just wanted to run away. I tried explaining the situation to my mum, but she thought I was exaggerating, and told me not to be so sensitive.

" But ma, the bosses son is always getting on tae me fir nothing, " I said hoping she would understand my predicament, and perhaps give me some advice. Or a wee cuddle would have been nice. Who am I kidding?

" It'll get better, remember they hev a business to run, and they canny afford some wee lassie hinging on tae ther apron strings aw the time, " she said abruptly as she walked past me towards the TV set, and proceeded to change to another channel.

" Thanks fir understanding, " I said sarcastically under my breath as I walked out the room.

Mum must have seen the tears well up in my eyes. She knew how upset I was, but she dismissed my feeling without even a single word of comfort. I know it has never been in her nature to show any affection, but unfortunately my brain has never quite managed to accept her detachment.
How can she be so cold, and ignore a cry for help from her only daughter. Why can't she break out of her suit of armour, and show me that she cares? Mum's reaction, although expected, simply magnified my problem, and made all my troubles even more difficult to deal with.
Her constant lack of affection always evokes a very strong feeling of rejection within me, causing me more heartache. It's a feeling that I could do without. And, for my own survival I have to blank out mum's lack of concern, as I find it far too upsetting to bear. I just can't comprehend WHY? She never says anything encouraging. Or why she just can't reach out, and give me a big HUG?
If only she was a bit more like Linda's mum. She cuddles, and kisses Linda all the time, and there doesn't NEED to be a reason. I wish Linda's mum would adopt me then all my problems would be solved. If only...

CHAPTER 6

Saturdays

Saturday was for us the best day of the week. Linda and I would happily jump onto a double-decker bus, and set off for Glasgow city centre. We just loved to go window-shopping, Hunting for any bargains in the ladies department, and also taking stock of all the latest fashion ideas that had just arrived on the rails.

Linda and I would walk along Argyle Street; into Etam's; Wallis's; and then saunter further up the Street past Lewis's one of Scotland's biggest department stores, but a bit old-fashioned for us swinging teenagers. No, we preferred C&A. who seem to be galloping ahead in the fashion stakes. And always at a reasonable price.

Glasgow was always extremely busy on Saturdays, but that was all part of the excitement. We loved the buzz. Our routine was to squeeze in as many of our favourite shops that we could possibly fit into one Saturday

" Linda, ah'm needing new shoes tae go we that new dress ah bought last week, " I said as we got off the bus.

" Och, ah thought ye were taking that frock back? " She said looking a touch confused.

" Naw! Ah'm keeping it, tae annoy ma maw, She things it's far too short. " I sniggered.

" Aye well, ah'm saying nothing, " Linda giggled as she spoke.

Saxone for us was the best shoe shop in the whole of Glasgow, although sometimes Saxone's shoes could be a bit pricey. But they were worth all the extra money, not because of the good quality of the leather. No! No! It was for the style of the shoe. It had to be the latest FASHION! Item to match our new outfits.

After doing all our homework on the shops merchandise we would wait until we had saved up enough money, then we knew exactly where to go, but we still couldn't resist checking out all the shops again, just in case we overlooked something special or missed a sale before parting with our hard earned money.

After our jaunt around the shops, we would end up absolutely starving. We never ate whilst we were shopping we just couldn't afford the distraction of eating. Linda and I were dangerously serious shoppers. But when our stomachs started to rumble, that's when we would put a halt to our shopping trip. And then quickly set off in the direction of our much-loved fish, and chip shop. It's called the Blue Lagoon, and it's situated under the bridge in Argyle Street known to Glaswegians as the HEILANMAN'S! Umbrella.

Our order never changed we always had a fish tea, which consisted of fish, and chips; White bread with plenty of real butter. Tea was also included in the price, but because we were regulars we were allowed coke a cola instead of tea, with no extra cost to the bill.

We just loved the Blue Lagoon. It was a cosy wee place with little booths, with red leather padded seats. None of the staff would put any pressure on us to rush our meal. Leaving Linda and I as much time as we wanted to chat away.

It had a great atmosphere, and we knew all the staff by their first names; they had become like an extension to our family. It was truly wonderful to have such a friendly place to go, and have a nice supper on a Saturday afternoon. We were at our happiest sitting in our own wee booth; drinking gallons of coke, and catching up on all the latest gossip of the week. Linda and I always felt at home, and sometimes I never wanted to leave, I could have stayed there forever.

" Hi girls, dae ye want a' the same as a' usual? "
Margaret the waitress asked in her half Glaswegian, half Italian accent as we sauntered in the door.

Margaret is a warm cheery forty something wee lady always smiling, a bit on the plump side. But, could you blame her, working in a fish, and chip shop all day must be a huge temptation especially when the chips are so good.

Margaret is very Italian looking with olive coloured skin, big ebony eyes, and jet-black hair set in the same curly style as my mum, looking like the rollers were still in her hair. But I think Margaret's curl is natural.

I'm certain Margaret is from Italian descent; she has a very strong foreign type accent mixed with a Glaswegian dialect.

" Aye, that's great Margaret, " Linda and I shouted at the same time.

" How's the job a' doing Patsy? " Margaret enquired as she showed us to our seats.

" Aye, aw right, but the bosses son is a bit o' ah pain in the old bazooka. "

" Well, ye can always hae a job here if yer a' stuck a'. "

" Thanks Margaret that's awfay kind o' ye, " I replied.
Margaret's dad, Geno was behind the counter putting more chips in the fryer.

" Och aye, Patsy, ye can hae a' job here ony time ye want a' one, " Geno shouted.

Geno is a handsome man for his age with a full head of thick white hair. He may be nearly seventy, but he is still a big sturdy good-looking man with a very distinguished appearance in his spotless white coat, and apron.
Geno also has a Glasgow ascent with a strong reference to Italy. He is a likeable man, and is always entertaining his waiting customers with his witty patter.

" Thanks Geno, ah might take ye up on that wan day. "

Sitting cosy in our wee booth, Linda and I blethered on for hours. She would tell me all about her school course, and although I longed to be studying too, I still loved to listen to Linda's stories, about the different students she had in her class. I didn't envy her one bit I knew Linda would one day make an excellent teacher. And I wished her every success.

No! My major resentment was with my mum and dad. They should have allowed me the opportunity to go to university with Linda, and we could have been on the same journey together. I really think I hate THEM!

Linda was well aware of the fact that I was really struggling with my new job. I had gone around to her house during the week, and I described the trouble I was encountering with the stupid telephone, and the nasty comments that Gordon is always making about my nervous ability when answering the phone. .

Linda was extremely angry with my bosses; she felt that I should have been given some training, and not just expected to be competent. Linda strongly argued that my employers were being neglectful by not giving me the support that I needed.

Sitting in the Blue Lagoon, Linda was trying her best to cheer me up. Suddenly I saw a glimmer of inspiration in her eyes. She picked up a spoon putting it directly onto her ear, and then she proceeded to use the spoon as a prop for a phone. Without any hesitation she jumped into the role of the unhappy customer, who was phoning up the office for information regarding a problem that she was having with her electricity.

" Hello! I want some wan tae come tae ma hoose tae fix ma lights, " she said coldly pretending to be angry, and trying her best not to laugh.

" Could you tell me what seems to be the problem? " I said politely quickly picking up a fork and using it as my imaginary phone, as I began to act out the scenario with Linda.

" Aye hen, it'll no go on, it's OOT! "   Linda said now struggling to hold on to her laughter.

" Alright then you give me your name, and address and tell me when it would suit you for one of our electricians to call, " I said without any hesitation.

" The NOO!! " Linda said in a controlled voice.

" I'm afraid all our electricians are out on calls at the moment, but as soon as one becomes available I'll sent him round, " I said in a very posh voice.

" Hey that's great hen. Thanks, " Linda said loving every minute.

" No problem, bye, " I said satisfied with my response.

" You did great Patsy, " Linda was now laughing out loud.

And I couldn't contain myself any longer. We were both slightly hysterical, but it was due to the magic of the moment. Our laughter could be heard all over the café, but we didn't care we were never lectured on the noise. The Blue Lagoon was accustomed to our hilarity. But when the hysteria was over, my heart began to sink; I remembered far too quickly that we were just playing a game, and that I still hadn't mastered the phone at all.

And on Monday morning I had to face it all again. I could feel my mood PLUNGE!

" LINDA, Oh! Linda! It's no use I get all flustered when its for real I don't THINK!! I'll ever get the hang o' it, " I said getting very frustrated, and angry with myself.

" Listen Patsy, I know you, and you could do anything if you put yer mind to it. You're a determined lassie; don't let the phone or that little shit bag Gordon get you down" Linda said, full of enthusiasm for my character.

" Ah know, ah know, yer right, " I slowly pondered over what Linda had said.

And Linda was right; I had to give myself a shake and start looking on the bright side, and not let this job beat me. I needed to start thinking positively. I know I have, excellent typing skills, and Jean the supervisor is always complimenting me on my good bookkeeping. I just had to come to grips with that blasted phone, and not let Gordon's nasty remarks upset me. Easier said than done. But I've got to be strong, and not let that wee bully Gordon WIN!
Linda is a great pal. I was desperate for someone to lift my mood, and steer me in the right direction. And Linda has been successful; she has managed to build up my confidence giving me the boost, that I needed so badly, which is vital for my survival, and peace of mind.
I was pleased that I felt so much better after our heart to heart, and our wee bit of play-acting. I have decided it's best to put it all behind me, and not let it spoil our weekend. Linda and I left the Lagoon, and headed back to the bus station to catch our bus home.

Singing, one of the Beatles songs in harmony, arm in arm as we walked.

" She loves …Yeah! Yeah! " With a tiny skip in our STEP!

Linda and I are going to the pictures tonight to see a double feature, " Madame X " and " Imitation Of Life ". Madame X is a tale about a woman married to a wealthy businessman. Her life is compromised by the accidental death of a man who had been romantically pursuing her. She is then forced by her mother-in-law to assume a new identity to save the reputation of her husband, and infant son. She wanders the world to forget her heartbreak with the aid of alcohol, and unsavoury men. Eventually, returning to the city of her downfall, she then murders a blackmailer who threatens to expose her past
Amazingly her now adult son who has become a Public Defender represents her in court. Hoping to continue to protect her son, she refuses to give her real name, and is known in the court as Madame X. What a heartbreaker!
Imitation of life, tells the story of a young white struggling actress with a six-year-old daughter. She meets a coloured widow and her light skinned eight-year-old daughter at the beach. This coloured lady is also finding it hard to make ends meet. The actress offers the widow a place to stay in return for some domestic duties. When the widow's daughter grows up, she rejects her mother because of her colour, and pretends to everyone that she is white. This causes her mother, who could only be described as a saint, endless heartache.
Both films are being shown in the Odeon at Eglington Toll, which is only a fifteen-minute walk from our house.
The leading lady in these two movies is Lana Turner. Lana is a convincing actress, but a touch over done in the

make-up department; she's a cross between Marilyn Monroe, and Danny La rue. A very young Sandra Dee is the daughter of Lana Turner in the movie Imitation of Life. We've heard from some of our friends that they are fantastic movies, but real tearjerkers so we'll need to bring plenty of hankies.

OH! If only Saturdays could last forever...

CHAPTER 7

Monday!!!

Monday morning came far too soon. But I had finally made my mind up over the weekend, and after the much appreciated therapy from Linda. I had finally come to the conclusion that I definitely needed to grasp the technique of talking to customers correctly, and not let that bloody phone, or scumbag Gordon beat me.

Instead of panicking all the time, it was crucial that I listen, and concentrated on my answer. I was sure I could carry it off if I used my posh voice, just like when I was acting in the Blue Lagoon with Linda. With the very first caller that morning I sprang into action, and confronted my terror. And I was pleasantly surprise to find it was easier than I expected. To my delight the customer actually appeared happy, and even thanked me for the information I had given him.

After several more successful calls, I started to relax, and even began to enjoy myself. And I knew. AT LAST! I had conquered my fear. What a relief!

A few weeks later, and when the dreadful horror of the phone had gone entirely, I actually began to enjoy my work a little. I could now quite effortlessly interact with Jean, and Wilma who also worked in the office.

But Gordon was still an irritating nuisance I had to deal with. He continued to complain about the standard of my work. Always asking questions to see if he could catch me out on something. And he didn't seem pleased that I was now coping with the phone. Thank God! He's not in the office every day.

Jean is the supervisor, and she has been working with the firm the longest. She is twenty-one, and has been with the office since she left school at fifteen. She is a married lady, with a little girl called Michelle. Jean is an attractive young woman with natural platinum blond hair, and unusual piercing grey blue eyes. She wears her beautiful hair tied up in a French roll.

Jean's placid nature makes her very approachable, and really easy to talk to, and she has a great sense of humour to hoot! I really like her.

I could tell by the expression on Jean's face that she wasn't pleased, and that she felt very uncomfortable when Gordon was bossing me about. And a couple of times she actually interrupted, and explained that it was the customer who had been in the wrong. Jean is extremely competent at her job, and Gordon is clearly aware of Jean's ability, and her highly professional skills, which she uses to manage the office so efficiently.

Gordon obviously respects her judgement, and he would let the matter drop in an instance if Jean interfered in any of the disputes, he was having with me. It felt so good not to be alone, and to have someone else in my corner.

Wilma, was the office junior before me, but she has now been promoted to clerkess. She is nineteen with a mop of red curly hair that she doesn't seem to be able to control. She has to tie it up very tightly with a thick rubber band. And I'm positive that it would be like a volcano exploding if that band BURST! Sending all her flame coloured hair out into the atmosphere.

Wilma is a pretty girl when she smiles, but sadly that doesn't seem to happen very often. She is also proficient at her job, but she doesn't seem to want to interact with me on any level. She never initiates conversation, and only speaks to me when answering a question.

But when Mr. Marshall senior, or Gordon come into the room, she could have easily won an Oscar for her performance. Her whole personality changes, her smile never leaves her face. She becomes Miss Sweetness, and Light whilst they are there but once they have left the room, then she quickly reverts back to Miss SOURPUSS again. I find it amusing to watch her performance. But sometimes I wished she would like me a just tiny bit!

At lunchtime Jean and I would sit, and chat. Jean would tell me all about her little girl Michelle, who had just, became two years old a couple of weeks ago. And it was obvious she loved talking about her. Looking into her eyes I could sense by the pining expression on her face, just how much Jean was missing her baby girl.

" Patsy, Michelle is learning tae go tae the potty at the minute, but she keeps picking it up, and putting it on her head, I think she thinks it's a hat. "

" That's cute, " I said smiling.

" I'm glad ye think so, but it's not so cute when she's wetting the floor. "

I felt a bit sorry for Jean, her husband was out of work so she had no choice, but to work full time. I'm certain Jean would rather have been at home, spending time looking after her precious little girl.
During our lunch break, I'd update Jean on what I was up to at the weekend, and tell her all about my best pal Linda. It was great having someone to talk to, which helped to take some of the pressure out of my work, and the chitchat was a welcome distraction from Gordon. Jean was just the tonic I needed to get me through the day.

" Linda and I went tae the pictures on Saturday night, we knew it was going tae be a weepy film, but we still weren't prepared for how heartbreaking it was going tae be. We almost used up a whole packet of hankies in the first movie " Madame X. " And we thought that the next film " Imitation Of Life " would be a wee bit less tragic, but we were wrong. It wis WORSE! I thought we might get thrown oot o' the theatre, because we were making such a racket, we aw oor greeting. What an embarrassment at the end o' the film we had tae go tae the toilets, and wash the black mascara off oor faces, " I said jovially.

" Patsy sounds like ye hid a brilliant night, " Jean said laughing at my predicament.

Wilma always went out for lunch. She didn't live in the city, therefore she couldn't go home, and be back in an hour, which was the length of time we had to spend. Jean, and I were really curious as to where Wilma went during her break.

Jean explained that Wilma didn't always go out for lunch, and she only started going out a few weeks before I came to work in the office. After some debate, Jean and I have come to the same conclusion; that Wilma has a boyfriend. We have even secretly discussed following her just to see what he was like. But decided it was far better not knowing because we could always use our imagination, and have a laugh.

" Maybe he has a mop of red hair too, " laughed Jean.

" Or maybe he's bald? " I said joining in the hilarity.

" Aye; or maybe he's only got one leg. "

" Or it could be she just disnae want tae hev her lunch we me? " I said changing the tone.

" Patsy, can ah be serious for a second, I know yer finding it rough at the moment with Gordon always on yer back. But Wilma is a very shy girl; it took her months before she would make any conversation at all. She wouldn't even talk tae me. Dinnae take her quietness personally be patient. It's jist Wilma's nature. I don't think she purposely means tae be unpleasant to ye, " Jean said trying to emphasize her point of view.

" But, Jean, she's not so quiet when Mr Marshall, or Gordon are on the scene, " I said a bit confused.

" I know, but that's a new thing. Maybe it's because she knows them longer? " Jean said defending Wilma.

BUT! My gut feeling is that, Wilma doesn't like me, and my granny Stewart said always go we yer gut instinct hen. But I will give Wilma the benefit of the doubt, only because I trusted Jean's opinion.

CHAPTER 8

Boyfriends

I can't believe that a year has gone so quickly, and it's now approaching the end of 1968. Linda and I are both now sixteen, and we are looking forward to the New Year ahead. It's been a long, and difficult year adjusting to my new life, but things seem to be settling down at work, making it more agreeable, I do, sometimes, hunger for knowledge, and the dream of becoming a teacher. But I'm learning to accept that in life we can't ALL have what we want.

It seems like only yesterday, that Linda and I were meeting up with the old gang after school, and just hanging about the street talking or playing football. But now that I'm working, and Linda has her studying, we never seem to have the time anymore to catch up with our mates. Part of our old life was rapidly fading away without us even noticing that it had gone.

Linda and I started going to a youth club every Friday night, held in the local St. Albert's church hall, which is only a few streets away. It is our first real taste of listening to live bands, and we were both blown away with the music, and the fantastic atmosphere of the venue. The bands were always extremely loud causing the room to vibrate with the sound. But it was an amazing experience, and one that we wanted to repeat over, and over again.

We do have boyfriends now, and again, but nothing serious. Linda and I would have everlasting love, long term for a whole two weeks. And it was definitely undying love for the first week, and then it was into the second week with a sudden change of emotions. Oh! GOD! What am I going to do? How do I tell him that I don't love him anymore, and it's all over?

It was never a simple task to end a relationship, and one, which we both hated, and we found very embarrassing. BUT! Sometimes, the guys had the upper hand, and it was US who were being dumped, and that was a real bitter pill to swallow, because then your pride is crushed, and you start to convince yourself he could have been the ONE!

But afterwards in our bedrooms, we had loads of fun dissecting our former boyfriend's clothes; hair; shoes; and their personality were all taken to pieces.

" Patsy, did ya no see his shoes? " Linda asked.

" Naw, whit wis wrang we them? " I said wondering where this conversation was leading.

" They were broon. "

" Well, whits a metter we that? " I asked still unsure what Linda was getting at.

" Broon shoes we bright red socks, naw ah could nae go oot we onybody dressed like that. "

" Linda, it wis nae his shoes ah wis worried aboot, it wis his eyes, wan o' his eyes wis looking straight at me, and the other wan wis looking tae see whit wis coming roon the corner. " We both howled with laughter. Almost peeing oor breeks.

During the week we would listen to music at Linda's house, and attempted to emulate some new dancing routines that we saw Pan's People create on Top Of The Pops. Then we would dance to Lulu's " Shout " and struggle to do the " shake ". Putting our bodies into weird positions, and almost straining all our muscles in an effort to master the dance. And you can imagine the sound of us singing at the top of our voices. Totally out of tune.

" SHOUT! SHOUT! Hey Hey Hey Hey, Hey Hey Hey Hey, " squealing out the words as we danced.

Linda's parents were great at allowing us the freedom to have our music blaring, as we jump about like silly kids. Making more noise than a herd of elephants stampeding in the jungle, leaping around to the beat of the music.
My mum, and dad would have freaked out if Linda and I had tried out one of our dances in their house. They could never have coped with any disruption in their wee flat. But I guess we did always have the neighbours to consider. Whilst Linda's family were fortunate to live in a detached house, where they didn't have to worry about upsetting anyone.

Linda's dad was a policeman, a tall stern looking man. Who appeared on the onset to be a bit bossy, but when you got to know him that part of his character melted away. Leaving behind a lovely gentle man, who was always ready to help if needed. Linda was so lucky she had her dad eating out of her hand.

" Da, can ah borrow yer camera fir ma project at college. Please dad can ah, " Linda asked.

" Aye, pet but mind ye take care o' it? " He said without any hesitation.

" Thanks dad yer a pal, " Linda said taking the camera, and giving her dad a kiss on the cheek.

And it was a very expensive Kodac camera too. My dad would have ignored my plea, and he would have given me a look that meant " ar ye aff yer heid?."

Linda's mum was a real gem; she had the same shinny jet-black hair as Linda, but cut short with a flick at the bottom. She, is so good-natured, and just never seems to stop smiling. I think Linda's mum and dad had lots of problems trying to have kids. And because they only had one child, Linda was spoiled rotten. But, give Linda her due, she never takes advantage of the situation, and is always very respectful to her mum, and dad.

Saturday was still our day for the town. Shopping, then going for our delicious fish tea at the Blue Lagoon. The highlight of our conversation, at the moment, was planning our first summer holiday together, without any mums or dads coming along, and interfering with our fun.

Linda and I knew we couldn't go anywhere for a couple of years, because we didn't have the money, plus our parents would never allow us to go until we were at least eighteen. But there was nothing stopping us saving, and planning where we wanted to go.

Linda and I spent hours, and hours blethering on about how great it was going to be getting away for two weeks on our own without our parents breathing down our necks, it would be heaven.

But! We still had to tell them, and get them to agree to let us go. And, we also had to decide where we wanted to go.

" Whit aboot going abroad tae Spain, or Italy? " Linda suggested.

" That wid be great, but I don't think we wid be able tae afford it, " I replied.

" Well then whit aboot... England? " Linda said a bit hesitant.

" But where...? " I replied unsure as I had never been anywhere outside Scotland.

" Ah don't know. "

" I think we need tae get oor selves some books on holidays. What do ye think? "

" Aye, that's a brilliant idea, " agreed Linda, all excited.

We left the Blue Lagoon early, and set off for the travel agents to get some brochures to help us plan our holiday of a lifetime...

CHAPTER 9

Gordon's Change Of Character

At the office Gordon suddenly changed his tactics, and instead of complaining constantly about my work he suddenly began to give me compliments. And the transformation of his character was incredible.

" Your doing a grand job Patsy, I'm really proud of you, keep up the good work. "

" Thanks, Mr. Marshall, " I said, but obviously startled by this sudden change of behaviour, and cautiously wondering why he was being so nice?

" Please, call me Gordon, " he said smiling.

" Oh! I'm not sure if that's acceptable, Mr Marshall? " I said struggling with this new image of Gordon.

" Of course it is Patsy, I'M giving you permission, " he said grinning.

WOW!!! Gordon is actually smiling at ME! At last I had finally managed to be proficient enough at my job to satisfy Gordon expectations. Clearly thinking, I had succeeded, and that Gordon had now transformed into a decent human being, and he evidently regretted treating me so badly, I invariably began to enjoy my work more, and to my astonishment I even started to like Gordon just a little.

It made my job a whole lot easier, and I was at last, happy to be at work. And with less time at home I was also able to miss out on my mum, and dad arguing which was great. Life was looking healthier than it had ever been in a long time, and the yearning to become a teacher was now less significant.

I'm sorry to say this high never lasted very long. Gordon was very subtle in his initial approach lingering his fingers very softly on my hand when I was passing him any letters, or he would brush against me not completely touching, but so uncomfortably close to me that I could feel his breath on the back of my neck as he stood behind me.

He was playing games with my head putting my mind off balance, and confusing my thoughts. At first I thought I was imaging it, but I knew deep down something wasn't quite right.

He was always very careful not to expose himself blatantly in case someone in the office noticed anything strange. Obviously this was making me feel very anxious, and flung me out of sync. All I could do to alleviate the problem was to avoid him as much as I possible. And for the first time in my whole life I was wishing I had my mum's talent, with her BIG! Mouth.

His suggestive behaviour went on for a few months, I never told anyone not even Linda; I can't explain, I don't quite know why? But I somehow felt I was to blame. I knew this was crazy, but I couldn't help myself.

But as the weeks turned into months I was beginning to get really worried as I felt that he was becoming more, and more daring, and I didn't know how to handle the situation anymore.

Never before in my entire life have I felt so scared. I wasn't coping; he was wearing me down. Why was he doing this to ME? He had a girlfriend, and he was supposed to be getting married next year. Why couldn't he just leave me alone?

Linda and I were sitting in the Blue Lagoon on Saturday after our usual trek around the shops. When Linda suddenly questioned my quietness, and my lack of concentration.

" Hev ye changed yer mind aboot the holiday is that whits wrang we ye? " Linda said sounding a bit annoyed.

" No! No! It's no that I can't wait tae go, a'm just tired, " I said waking up out of my trance state.

" Your miles away Patsy, whit's up wee ye? " Her voice changed, and was now soft and low filled with concern.

" Its nothing I'm just tired, " I lied again.

" There's sumthing wrong! I know YOU: Yer no yer sell.

Ye hev nae been right fir weeks, tell me whit it is? I'm worried aboot ye Patsy, " she said tenderly.

Linda was waiting patiently for me to answer her question. Her eyes were studying my face. Oh GOD! I didn't know where to start, but before I could utter another word the tears just poured out. I couldn't hold back any longer. I couldn't blank it out any more I had to face up to what was happening, and try to make some sense of it.
But! I was so ashamed, I felt so guilty, and I didn't want to tell anyone not even Linda. I was blaming myself; I smile too much; I'm too friendly; I sometimes give the wrong impression; I had lost all logic.
When I was rational, I was confident that I wasn't to blame for Gordon's deplorable behaviour. I needed to confide in Linda. I was desperate for her advice, more than ever before. I needed her to help me before I went crazy. I took a big gulp of air before I started to speak.

" Well ye know how ah told ye that Gordon wis a changed character, and he wis actually being nice tae me?"

Slowly I plucked up the courage to disclose the burden that was driving me mentally insane.

" Aye...aye... "

" Well...it's Gordon; he's... He keeps touching me up at any opportunity, " I blurted out.

Linda was visibly shocked, her mouth opened wide, and her chin hit her chest, and she didn't say a word. She was obviously gobsmacked. She got up from her seat, and gave me a big hug, but that made me more upset. My tears came flooding, and we were getting some funny looks from customers. We decided to make a quick exit out of the door avoiding passing Margaret.

" Patsy, are ye aw right? " Margaret shouted from the other side of the room.

" Aye, Margaret nothing tae worry aboot. Patsy's jist got sumthing in her eye, see ya next week, " Linda shouted back as she guided me through the door.

" Aw well, see ya a' next week, " Margaret said looking puzzled at our very hurried departure, and maybe a touch in the huff at not being included in what was obviously upsetting me.

I told Linda the whole story on the way home. I explained how at first I thought it must be a figment of my imagination, and that my mind was playing tricks on me. Then I began to feel guilty thinking I had done something to give him the impression I was happy for him to treat me this way.

" I must be doing sumthing tae encourage him, " I said hesitantly.

" WHIT! Am I going tae dae we ye. You could never encourage sumd'y like him, " Linda emphasized raising the tone of her voice.

" Whit am ah going tae DAE? " I said with a mixture of anger and despair. I was now staring into Linda's face waiting on a response. Hoping she could solve my problem in an instance.

" Gees a minute tae think. "

" No one will ever believe me. He is very calculated in what he does He is a perfect gentleman when he has an audience, but when we are out of sight then he makes his move, " I said with conviction, and relieved to be pouring out all my fears to Linda.

Linda was silent for what seemed like an eternity. She was deep in thought, and was obviously concentrating on what she was going to say to me. Finally she had reached a conclusion, and began to speak. She turned towards me, and held my shoulders in both hands, and she looked straight into my eyes. She paused for a second, and took a deep breath, and then she slowly, and meticulously explained.

" Patsy, I think ye hev tae get oot o' that place, and get another job as quickly as ye can. Yer no going tae win this wan. He's the boss's son. His faither will defend him tae the hilt, even if he knows Gordon is guilty. Mr Marshall will protect his son regardless of what he thinks of you. I'm convinced ye should go as soon as possible before Gordon becomes too demanding, and ye are unable to control the situation, " Linda said all grown up before my eyes.

" Aye, yer right, " I said accepting Linda's proposition, and giving her a big hug for being so understanding, and never doubting my character for even a second.

Linda was spot on with her conclusion. I had to find a new job, and I had to start looking immediately. I scanned the papers that night when I went home. There weren't any suitable office jobs for me at the rate of pay I was receiving. I had to find a position that paid the same wage or more to keep mum happy. It would cause a lot of trouble if I had to reduce her dig money.

There was a job for a dressmaker's assistance at the King's Theatre in Glasgow that paid the same rate. I didn't have time to be fussy. I phoned on the off chance, and asked to speak to a Mrs. Henry whose name was in the advert. My luck was in. Mrs. Henry was available to come to the phone.

She asked me if I could sew, and I immediately answered, " Yes. " Good! Could you come along Saturday morning at ten o'clock for an interview? I happily agreed to attend.

I couldn't wait to tell Linda. I was totally wired up with excitement. I could hardly contain myself. But then the reality hit me, and brought me back down to earth. What on earth was I thinking! I couldn't SEW!

By the time I saw Linda that night I was completely deflated. I was now convinced I was wasting my time. There was no way on this planet I was going to get this job. It was hopeless. I was slowly becoming depressed at the mere thought of having to face Gordon everyday. I knew I needed to get out of that environment before it really affected my health.

Linda listened to my news, and was delight at the prospect of me finding a new job. She was now totally aware of the anguish I was enduring, and the torture of being in the same office as Gordon every day. Linda was eager for me to get this new job, and not being able to sew according to Linda wasn't a big problem.

" Look Patsy, don't upset yerself, at the interview just exaggerate the skills ye hev, and admit that ye don't hev aw the skills needed, but that yer keen tae learn. And remember tae lie aboot how much ye want the job, " Linda said with confidence.

" WHIT! Are ye mad? " I said nervously.

" Did yer granny no teach ye how tae suck eggs? Well this is the time tae sell yerself. As Miss I can do Onything," Linda replied with enthusiasm, and a hint of laughter.

We both took one look at each other then burst out laughing. Thank GOD! She had the knack of making me laugh, especially when all the chips were down, which always made me feel so much better. What would I do without her??

When Linda had gone home I lay on my bed, and for just a fleeting second I pondered over approaching mum and telling her what's been happening with Gordon, but despite the fact that I would have loved to have mum's support on my side I knew I couldn't risk it.

No, I'm far too scared to tell her what's been happening, and I'm just not prepared to take a chance, in case she defends Gordon. And the disappointment if she chose NOT to believe ME would be DEVASTATING! And far, far too much for me to bear.

No I can't afford a bad reaction from mum. It would totally destroy me. No, it's better if I say nothing.

Although I don't really want to I am slowly learning to keep my distance from mum, and I'm building up a barricade to keep me safe. It's the only way I know to survive...

CHAPTER 10

The Interview

I deliberately avoided Gordon all week, and every time I saw him coming towards my desk I would swiftly leave my seat, and go into the toilet. Or walk over to Jean's desk, and pretend I needed her help with an order, or simply borrow a pen. Making numerous excuses to keep him at bay. I'm not sure if the girls noticed my erratic behaviour. But I had no choice.

It was an extremely tough week trying to stay out of Gordon's way. But having the slightest possibility of being accepted for this new job at the King's Theatre has given me the hope I need to help me cope with this grim situation.

Saturday came at last, and I had a whole two days away from Gordon what a RELEIF! Linda and I set off at nine o'clock so we would be at the King's Theatre before ten. I didn't want to be late. I knew how important it was to make a good first impression.

It was also fortunate for me that the interview was on Saturday, and I didn't have to make any excuses, or take any time off from work, which could have been awkward in the circumstances. It also meant Linda was able to come along, and keep me sane.

I hardly slept last night. I kept going over, and over in my head what I was going to say at the interview. I still hadn't a clue how I was going to approach the situation. But I did know I had to convince this lady, I was the best candidate for the job. I desperately needed her to employ me.

Linda and I were now standing outside the King's theatre. I felt so nervous, and I couldn't stop my hands from shaking. I wore a navy blue suit, and a white shirt, which I had bought last year for our office Christmas dinner. I also had my favourite navy paten shoes on that I just loved to bits (bought from Saxone' of course). My hair was swept back pinning some up, and leaving the rest down.

I looked the part, but could I convince this Mrs. Henry, that I was the right person for the job, and hopefully make her believe that my BIG passion in life has always been to become a dressmaker.

OH! I do hope so.

I walked through the large doors of the King's theatre into the foyer. And I was suddenly transported into a different world. I had never been inside the King's before, and the first thing that struck me was the massive arched ceiling, and the beautiful carvings on the walls. In the middle of the room is a huge white marble staircase with a deep red coloured carpet running up the centre of the steps leading straight into the theatre. What a welcomed sight for the customer's who come through those doors.

There was definitely a magical atmosphere inside this spectacular building, and I could feel the enchantment engulf my mind.

The doorman was standing at the foot of the stairs, and he smiled as he walked towards me. After introducing himself he asked me if I would follow him back stage. He then escorted me to a room where a lady in her forties was sitting behind a desk obviously waiting for me to arrive. When I entered she immediately stood up, and introduced herself as Sylvia Henry. Then she very politely offered me a seat.

Sylvia has short black hair cut in a Mary Quant bob style. She is a very pretty lady with large hazel eyes. She is tall, and elegant with an apparent pleasant nature, and when she smiled her whole face lit up exposing her Shirley Temple dimples. I liked her instantly.

Sylvia then proceeded to ask me some details about my present job, my family, and where I lived. I felt quite relaxed in her presence, and able to talk freely. When all the formalities were dealt with, she said very calmly.

" Tell me Patsy, what experience do you have, and why do you want to be a dressmaker? "

This was my moment! And I had to sell myself. I had been thinking about what I was going to say all week. And I now had to sell my big lie.

I explained that " I was my granny's only granddaughter, and that she was a brilliant dressmaker. She made all her own clothes, and she also made clothes for our neighbours, and their kids, and when I was wee she made all my dresses. Oh, and I nearly forgot she made my Aunty Joan's wedding dress, which was just the most beautiful dress that I have ever seen. She taught me how to sew, and my dream is to be as good a dressmaker as she was.

My only regret would be, she is not alive to witness my success," I quickly added.

My face was the colour of beetroot, and I could feel the heat travel downwards reaching my toes. I hope, Mrs. Henry doesn't see through my unbelievable scam, and with any luck regards my embarrassment as nerves.

I did however manage to muster up a lot of genuine emotion into my reply hoping for a sympathy vote. I focused all my sentiment on my gran hoping the sincerity of my love would camouflage my lies. My granny died went I was ten years old, leaving behind a huge void in my life.

I loved my granny Stewart with all my heart, and it wasn't all lies she did try to teach me how to sew on a toy sewing machine once! But it was a DISASTER! Between us we tried to make clothes for my dolls, but we never managed to make anything that resembled dolls clothes. Granny, and I would always end up with a bag of rags. But we did have a lot of fun trying.

Sylvia thanked me for coming. She explained that there were still some more applicants to interview, but she would let me know in a day or two.

Linda was waiting outside, and as soon as she saw me. She waved her hand, and then ran across the road to greet me.

" Well! How did it go? " She said impatiently dancing on the spot waiting on my reply.

" Ah don't know. Ah did ma best. Ah told the biggest lies of my entire life, " I said unsure now that the interview was over if I had done the right thing, and still feeling extremely embarrassed at telling so many lies.

" Great! That's exactly whit ye were suppose tae dae, " Linda enthused.

" Linda I lied I said that my granny made me beautiful dresses, and that she even made my aunty Joan's wedding dress, and she taught me how to sew. I also told her my big dream was to be a dressmaker like my granny Stewart. Oh! If she only new the truth?"

" Don't worry she disnae need tae know the truth, " Linda encouraged.

" My granny could nae sew a button on a coat, and ma Aunty Joan's has never been merried, she's been looking fir a husband aw her life, " I started laughing hysterically, releasing all the tension in my body caused by the anxiety of the interview.

Linda took one look at my flushed face, and joined in the laughter. We laughed, and laughed until we forgot what we were laughing about.
Travelling back on the bus after a good day shopping, and our usual fish supper. My mind was suddenly jolted back to reality. And the thought of going back to work on Monday made me lose all my concentration.

" Ah, might buy that...bla, bla, bla... " Linda was chatting on and on.

I tried really hard to listen to what Linda was talking about. But my mind kept wandering, and the sound of Linda's voice was muffled into the background. All I could think about was being stuck in that office, and never ever being free.

Trapped, and terrified of having to be anywhere near Gordon. I dreaded the thought of going back to work on Monday, and my heart was becoming heavy once again.

OH! God! What if I never get another job...

CHAPTER 11

Alone With Gordon

I had another troubled nights sleep on Sunday. Tossing, and turning in bed, constantly fighting with my pillows all night long. Aggravated, and frustrated trying fruitlessly to find a way to escape from all my problems, and then thinking I might have found a solution. But waking up to the realisation that I was only dreaming, and nothing had changed. I felt completely miserable, and absolutely exhausted.

I arrived at the office exactly on time. I didn't want to be a minute early, because I wanted to be entirely sure I wasn't alone in the office with Gordon. When I entered the girls were already busy behind their desks sorting out the job sheets for the electricians.

" Good morning girls, " I said as I entered the office, trying to sound cheerful. Making a huge effort to conceal my true feelings.

As the morning progressed Jean and Wilma started to complain that they didn't feel very well. Both of them were sneezing, and coughing constantly. Jean and Wilma had the same symptoms feeling hot one minute, and cold the next. It was obvious they had contacted some sort of virus.

Gordon came out of his office, and when he saw how ill Jean and Wilma were, he insisted that they should go home immediately.

" Girls you don't look well, I think you should both go home, " he said with compassion in his voice.

All of a sudden the circumstances were becoming potentially dangerous I was beside myself. What was I going to DO!!!! Mr. Marshall was away for the day, and I would be left all alone with Gordon. Oh! NO!!! As my mind slowly grasped the situation the reality set me reeling, and my heart was beating so fast I thought it was surely going to explode. I could pretend that I didn't feel well, in spite of the fact that I didn't have any apparent signs of an illness. Although, I did suddenly feel ill, and was certain I was about to throw UP!

Jean and Wilma would know I was lying, and assume that I just wanted a day off work. And I'm positive Gordon would suspect that I was insincere, and would do his utmost to stop me leaving.

But did I really CARE! What they thought or what Gordon thought I was DESPERATE; I needed to get out of the office FAST. I had to somehow think up an excuse.

But! WHAT???

As Gordon quickly arranged for a taxi to take the girls home I sat at my desk motionless, praying he wouldn't do anything when they had gone, and trying to convince myself that I would be safe.

And in those last precious minutes when Jean, and Wilma were preparing to leave I procrastinated, and I lost my CHANCE! Of ESCAPE! I wanted to run out that door. But I was somehow paralysed to the spot. I could feel the frustration well up inside of me. But still I sat there frozen. Franticly struggling in my head to come up with a plan to get away, and at the same time trying to convince myself, that I had nothing to worry about. I became extremely angry and annoyed with myself for not making more of an effort to leave the premises with the girls. My brain was screaming at me to GO! GO! GO! Get out QUICK!!!

But, I didn't. I just sat there immobile.

I was still desperately clinging on to the idea that he wouldn't do anything, and that I could possibly be over reacting. But at the same time my gut feeling was telling me I was right, and Gordon was NOT to be trusted.

Going out the door, Wilma was almost pleading with Gordon not to send her home, and I was hoping he would let her stay.

" How will you manage? " She said more disgruntled than normal.

" Me, and Patsy will be fine, " he said, almost with a hint of desire.

On her way out Wilma looked loathingly over Gordon' shoulder, throwing me a disgusted glare, as she walked out the door.

Good GOD! What had I done to HER! But I didn't have time to dwell on what could possibly be wrong with

Wilma. I was in a serious situation, and I had no idea how it was going to end.

I sat glued to my desk praying for a solution, but I still hadn't come up with any scheme to solve my predicament. It was impossible to think straight knowing that any minute now I would soon be left on my own with the SHITTY WEE GORDON!

It was eleven thirty when they left, and the girls were gone only minutes when Gordon announced that we could take an early lunch. HEY! Wait a second. Maybe! I was wrong after all.

I went into the toilet to get my coat, but on the way back Gordon was standing at the front door. What was he up to? Had he lock the door? These thoughts were circling in my head. When I reached the door, he continued to stand in front of the door blocking my exit.

" Wait, I need to talk to you first, " he said quietly.

Oh! GOD! What could he possibly want to talk about? My heart was racing. I wanted to run out the door, but he was obstructing my get-away. OH! MY! GOD! I was TRAPPED!

We both walked back slowly towards my desk. Gordon was behind me, painfully too close to my body, almost stepping on my heals, but before I got to the desk. He grabbed me, and swung me around to face him. My bag fell to the floor, and before I could utter a sound. His lips were on mine; his arms engulfing my body, holding me firmly against him like a vice; I tried to wrestle with him, but he just tightened his grip. His lips pressed hard over my mouth, I tossed my head from side to side in a frantic attempt to stop his mouth from touching mine. But I was no match against his strength.

All the time I was struggling Gordon was whispering in my ear not to be scared, and that there was nothing to worry about. Telling me he would look after me. He said he loved me from the first day he saw me.

He was repeating, " You know I love you, " again, and again.

I kept on dodging his advances for what seemed like forever. Eventually I couldn't fight him off any longer, I was completely worn out. Exhausted, I stopped fighting. He then started to kiss me very slowly smothering my mouth, almost stopping my breathing. Tears were rolling down my cheeks.

" Please, please let me go? " I said gasping for air.

" It's going to be all right, " Gordon said softly ignoring my pleas.

I kept my eyes closed. I couldn't look at him. I didn't want to see his ugly face.
My mind was reeling I didn't know what to do next. All my strength was draining away I was losing the fight.
OH! GOD! I had to beat HIM! Somehow; I had to fight back, and find that last bit of strength to break away from his hold.
I felt his hand touch my inner thigh, as he roughly pulled my skirt up to my waist. My mind was tormented. OH! NO! NO! PLEASE GOD! NO! I wanted to scream, but I couldn't my voice was paralysed I had lost all capability of making a sound.

I was DOOMED!

When suddenly there was a BANG! BANG! BANG! At the front door.

Gordon quickly put his hand over my mouth, pressing his fingers tight against my lips squashing them into my face, and scratching the inside of my mouth with his nails in a wild attempt to prevent me from uttering a sound. Little did he know the shock had already numbed my voice.

" Shush! Shush! " He said in a low threatening tone, his anger was evident in his evil eyes.

A woman's voice was shouting " Gordon! Gordon! Are you in there? "

BANG! BANG! BANG! Again " Gordon, it's me, Laura, " she shouted.

Gordon looked at me, and I could see his whole personality change instantly. He looked vexed. He pushed me hard towards the toilets. My body fell hard against the door, propelling me inside.

" GO, and wash your face, and don't breathe a WORD to Laura, " he said with a menacing sound to his voice.

I stood in the toilet looking in the mirror, but saw no reflection. I could not comprehend what had just happened. My brain still hadn't registered the incident, but I knew if I acted quickly I had an opportunity of escape, but I had to move very fast or I might lose the possibility.

I washed my face instinctively hoping for some reaction from the cold water as it touched my skin, but it was ineffective at that moment I was beyond help. My hands were shaking, but I had no time to calm myself, I had to get out of the office. NOW!!!

I walked out of the toilet over to my desk picked up my bag, and walked past Gordon, and Laura. I didn't say a word. I couldn't. I didn't know how! The ability to speak was gone. Laura gave me a puzzled look, but I was past caring.

As my eyes half focused on Laura, I felt a tinge of sadness for her; she is a sweet girl, very beautiful with big blue eyes, and a figure to die for. She deserves someone far better than Gordon. And for a fleeting second a small part of me wanted to warn her, but it would be hopeless. Laura would never believe ME!

Laura obviously has no idea that Gordon is a wee sleaze bag, and I could never be the one to tell her. And, WHY! Gordon would want to risk losing Laura is beyond me.

But at this moment, I didn't care what she thought about me. My only concern is to get as far away from the office, and Gordon as quickly as I could. I walked out that door and never looked back. The door closed automatically behind me. BANG!

Out in the street I wanted to cry out. To SCREAM! But, I couldn't all my senses were frozen. I went into autopilot. Jumping on the bus. Walking up the street. Climbing up the stairs. Making every effort to reach my home as quickly as I could. I had no recognition of time, or place, I was in a different world.

Once inside the house, I breathed a sigh of relief to find that mum had gone out. I went straight to my room, and as I lay on my bed, I curled up into a ball. I searched what thoughts I had left in my head, and tried to make some sense of what had happened, BUT! My brain failed to comprehend the magnitude of the incident, and I was now in no condition to reflect. All I could do was cry. I cried for what seemed like an eternity.

Then somehow I drifted into a deep sleep, and never stirred until I heard a door being open. I jumped up totally disorientated, and for a split second I thought that Gordon was still attacking me, and that I was still in the office. My heart was racing then I heard my mum shout, and I realised I was safe in my bed.

Mum was now home, I wanted to run to the kitchen, and tell her what had happened; I needed her to cuddle me, to hold me close to her, and tell me everything was going to be all right. But I couldn't. Sadly I remembered, she would never understand.

Then I realised it was still too early for me to be in the house. I would have to quickly think up some kind of an excuse about why I was home at three o'clock in the afternoon. But, under no circumstances could I ever tell her what happened.

I fumbled into my pyjamas, and housecoat, and walked slowly into the living room. My eyes were red, and puffy. I knew I didn't look good. I was still pale, and in shock.

" Ma I've been sent home. Everyone in the office has the flu, " I said pitifully.

" Aw hen, ye don't look well; away back tae yer bed, and I'll bring ye up a cup o' tea, " mum said looking quite concerned, and nearly convincing me that she really did care.

Watching her reaction, and feeling so vulnerable, I was almost tempted to tell her the whole pathetic story, but then I remembered this was my MUM! Standing in front of me. This woman; whom all of my life has never ever been able to show me even a tiny morsel of affection. Good GOD! I must be completely delirious to be considering confiding in mum of all people. I slowly dragged my feet out of the kitchen in a daze to return to the safe haven of my room. I lay on top of my bed not wanting to think preferring to blank out the nightmare.

After about ten minutes, mum came into my room with some tea and toast. She handed me a letter.

" Em...it came this efternin, " she said.

I scrutinised the letter. This could be my escape. But it was too much to hope for. My need was so great. I could be free of Gordon for good. I held the letter in my hand. I wanted to tear it open, but I hesitated: I was terrified that I might be disappointed, and delaying opening it meant, I could also delay losing the little hope I have left. So much now depended on me getting this new job.

I wasn't thinking straight. My brain was scrambled, and unable to fully appreciate the situation. I was vaguely aware that mum was still sitting on the bed, and after about five minutes of her twiddling her thumbs she finally blurted out her question.

" Patsy! Are ye no gonnae open the letter the noo? " Mum said obviously annoyed and confused at why I was taking so long to open the letter.

I could hear her voice in the distance, but I didn't know how to react. I felt as if I was about to fall down a black hole, and would never be able to get out, and the strange thing is I wanted to go. Oh GOD! I just wanted to let go. I could feel my body weakening. BUT! I didn't have the strength to stop myself from FALLING!

" PATSY! Patsy! Whits a matter we ye? "   My mum was shouting, and she was now violently shaking me trying to get a response.

I felt her hands on my shoulders, and my head moving backwards, and forward as she shook my weak body. Her loud voice was penetrating my brain driving me out of my trance like state, and forcing me to become conscious of my environment. I reluctantly prised opened my eyes, and saw my mum's worried face staring back at me. I don't know where I got the strength, but I forced myself to let go of these depressing feelings that were dragging me down.

The envelope was still in my hand. I tore it open, and removed the letter. I read it! I read it again! To be absolutely positive that it was for real, and I wasn't dreaming.

" Well! Whit des it say? " Mum said impatiently.

I jumped out the bed. Mum was now looking at me as if I was a crazy person.

" I got it. I got it! " I shouted, as loud as I could, as I dance around the room.

" Got whit? " Mum asked.

" Mum, I've got a new job, I'm going to be a dressmaker at the King's Theatre, " I screamed unable to contain my happiness.

" Whits wrang we the job yev got, " she said totally confused at my behaviour.

" This job has better prospects, and more money, " I lied.

" That's good thinking hen, its no use working fir pennies, when you can get pounds, " mum chanted.

If she only knew the real reason why I was leaving my job. But regrettably I could never confide in her, and risk any more anguish. I had been through enough for one day. But now, I was absolutely thrilled at the prospect of never having to face Gordon again. I was FREE!! FREE!!
Having a solution to my problems would help me; I know to get over the trauma of what happened with Gordon today. It won't make the memory disappear altogether, but it will help me on the road to recovery knowing I don't ever have to see his ugly face again. I feel my character is strong enough not to let some wee scum bag like Gordon damage my future. I can't let him WIN!
I phoned the office early the next morning hoping that Mr. Marshall would be there. I was extremely nervous, and I was terrified Gordon would pick up the phone. But I had to take the chance.
I waited impatiently for an answer to my call, but after what seemed like an eternity, I was relieved to hear the sound of Mr. Marshall's voice on the other end of the line. I nervously explained to him that I was sorry, but I had found a new job, and that it was one, which I had been in search of for a long time. I was careful not to tell him where my new employment was, just in case he told Gordon. I also revealed that I had not been feeling well, and that I thought I might have the same virus as Jean,

and Wilma, and therefore wouldn't be able to work my notice.

" Don't worry about that, just you take good care of yourself, and good luck with the new job, " he said sounding sympathetic.

" Thanks, good-bye, " I said relieved that he had not bombarded me with questions.

After talking to Mr. Marshall, I felt a bit guilty at leaving under these circumstances, but Gordon has left me no choice. I will miss Mr. Marshall. He appeared to be genuinely sorry to hear I was leaving, and he said he would give me a good reference. What a nice man. I could never tell him that his only son was a vile human being. It would break his heart.

I feel so sad that I won't be seeing Jean any more, she was always good to me, and she helped to train, and encourage me in my office duties. Maybe I should have confided in her? But again, I didn't want to get her involved. I know how much her family depends on the money she earns.

Unfortunately, Jean is the only breadwinner in her family, and I would feel responsible if she lost her job. I wouldn't want Jean to be on my conscience if Mr. Marshall were to sack her because of her friendship with me.

I only hope that one day in the future I will meet up with Jean again, and be able to explain the real reason I left without saying goodbye, and I can only hope she will be able to forgive me for my hasty departure.

CHAPTER 12

King's Theatre

I spent the rest of the week moping around my bedroom trying to blank out my horrible ordeal. I hadn't even bothered to wash or get dressed, and I hardly ate anything. I was feeling really depressed with recurrent flashbacks each night with dreadful images of me locked in the office, with Gordon's hands pressed tight around my throat squeezing all the oxygen out of my lungs, and his FACE! OH! GOD! HIS FACE! I would wake up in a cold sweat gasping for air feeling totally wrecked, and exhausted, but extremely relieved to find I was safe in my bed, and that I was just having another bad dream.

Linda did her utmost to lift my mood. She took the week off college to be with me, coming round every morning, encouraging me to get out of bed, and to at least wash my face, and forcing me to eat something. But most of all she was an ear for me to off load all of my bad thoughts. She listened to me ranting on, and on allowing me to get rid of my self-destructive feelings. I think Linda was really scared that I might do something silly. But thank god I have such a good friend. She's so good at putting everything into perspective, and making me look at all the positive aspects of my life.

" Ye hev tae start looking on the bright side Patsy an try tae blank it oot o' yer heed think yer sel lucky that Laura had came tae yer rescue or it could hev been a lot worse. He could hev raped ye, " Linda kept reminding me just how fortunate I had been.

" Aye ah know, ah know, " agreeing with her statement, but struggling to let the horrible flashbacks leave my head.

" Ma only regret is that the bugger's getting away we it. But ye never know he might get caught oot one day, " I could hear the angry tone in Linda's voice as she spoke.

Linda was right. I had a lucky escape, and now I had to put it in the past, and not let it take over my life. I had a new job, and a fresh beginning to look forward to. Things weren't that awful.
Mum kept doing her nosey. Chapping on my bedroom door every hour asking if I was all right. She was going crazy with curiosity desperate to know why Linda was coming to visit every day. It was obvious the way mum was creeping about outside that she probably had her ear glued tight against the door trying with all her might to listen to our conversation. She was extremely eager to find out if we were up to something.

"Linda yer going tae catch the flu if yer no careful, being stuck in this room aw day we aw Patsy's germs. " Mum queried as she watched us very suspiciously while she handed Linda and I a cup of tea.

" Och its aw right Mrs. Stewart a'h hid the flu last week, I'm immune tae it noo, " Linda lied with conviction.

" Well, ah still don't know why yer wanting tae sit in here aw day, " mum was not completely satisfied with Linda's answer.

As I watched mum leave the room, I felt a bit sorry that I hadn't confided in her. She was my mum after all, and she did look a bit hurt thinking we were planning some great big secret, and not including her. Perhaps I should call her back, and tell her the whole awful story.

I hesitated, I know I'm not strong enough to deal with an attack of my character, be it only words. Her criticism if she chose to chastise me could be the last straw. And anyway if she hadn't stopped me from following my dream, and had let me go to college with Linda, I wouldn't be in this terrible predicament. No! I can't take a gamble with my life.

By Saturday I was ready to leave the sanctuary of my room. Linda and I spent the entire day shopping. I bought a completely new outfit to cheer me up. And it worked! At the Lagoon, I showed Margaret my new clothes, and told her all about the new job at the King's. My spirits were high.

" That's a' great Patsy, but ah didnae know that ye kid a' sew, "explained Margaret, genuinely surprised at the revelation that I was going to be a dressmaker.

" A'h cannae, " I said with a snigger.

" But! How are ye a' gonnae manage aw the sewing? "

" I'll, jist brass neck it, and pretend to be brilliant, "

Margaret laughed at my plucky reply. Linda and I instantly joined in, and the laughter was just the wee tonic I needed to forget, and move forward with my life. I was now definitely on the road to recovery.

But when the hilarity had ceased, and I was back home that night getting ready for bed, and contemplating what I was expected to do in my new job. That's when the reality hit me, making me exceedingly nervous at the prospect of Sylvia finding out that I was a complete fraud.

Could you imagine me behind a sewing machine trying to make costumes for the stars? What a joke! It wasn't so funny anymore. Oh! GOD! What have I done? Maybe I should have told Sylvia the truth?

I didn't sleep very well on Sunday night. But it was a different kind of restlessness, not a terrible nightmare about Gordon, No! Just a bad dream thinking I was going to be exposed. I kept dreaming that I had made a mess of one of the leading lady's most expensive costume, and I was trying to hide my mistake. But there was nowhere to hide the BIG! Dress with all its layers. I tried to stuff it in a cupboard, but the material just kept springing out on top of me like a jack in the box. Every time I put it back in the cupboard it would pop out again. Ultimately I fell out of the bed and landed on the floor tangled up in my blanket.

I awoke scared, and startled by the fall, but pleased to find that I had been dreaming, and it was only the blankets that I had been fighting with. Thank GOD!

On my first day of starting at the King's, I didn't have to be at the theatre until ten o'clock. And the late start helped me recover from my poor nights sleep. I was still a bit nervous, and concerned that Sylvia might realise I didn't have the experience she was expecting, and the game would be up. I was fearful that I would be discovered immediately, and I that I was going to lose my job on the spot.

Sylvia was waiting for me in the costume room. She made me a nice cup of tea, and as I drank the really appreciated hot drink, Sylvia took her time to describe in detail what my duties would be. I felt so guilty drinking tea with this nice honest lady.

Sylvia gave me a piece of material, and a sewing machine to practice on. She granted me plenty of time to learn the skills of sewing, and the best part was, she didn't stand over me, which allowed me to learn on my own, and hide my incompetence.

As the day progressed, and my ability improved I was actually surprised at my fast development I was able to sew in straight lines, and all my fingers were still intact at the end of the day.

As the week progressed my technique improved and I was unexpectedly promoted to repairing costumes, which had been accidentally ripped at the seams during a performance. I could hardly believe how far I had come in just one week. I felt really important, and was getting carried away with the charismatic atmosphere of the King's Theatre.

At the end of the week Sylvia seemed really pleased with my progress. And I was relived that she hadn't discovered my big secret.

" Your a whiz Patsy! You're a fast learner, and a natural with the sewing machine. You're much better than I thought you would be. Your granny taught you well, and she would have been so proud of you, " she said smiling.

" Thanks, fir giving me this opportunity, " I replied.

But at that moment I felt a pang of guilt, and wished I hadn't lied about my granny Stewart. Someday I'll tell Sylvia the truth, but not just YET!
My expectations were now on a high, and I was becoming very excited at the possibility of repairing some of the celebrity's costumes. And I could PERHAPS! In the near future make a whole outfit for a leading lady or gent.

Hey, I can DREAM!

My first week was amazing. I was ecstatic, but worried that it wouldn't last. I couldn't be this jammy. I went round to Linda's that night to let her know I had managed to pull it off.

" I can't believe I'm happy at ma work, and nice people actually existed, " I told Linda.

" Ah, Patsy you deserve it, after all yev been through, " Linda said encouragingly.

" But, ma wan big concern was that the bubble would burst, and I'd find ma'sell wance mair in a situation which becomes so intolerable that I'd hev tae leave, " I said, feeling a bit depressed remembering how badly Gordon had treated me.

"RELAX! Patsy, ye got oot before onything serious happened! Ye hev tae pit it behind ye, and move on, " Linda said encouraging me to forget the past.

" Aye, Yer right! I need tae move ON! I've got a great job, and I don't hev tae see that shitty wee Gordon ever again," I said with anger in my voice.

" Plus ye can sew noo! Yer the new Pierre Cardin, " Linda fell onto the bed then rolled onto the floor holding her side as she fell, and her laughter spewing out of control.

" P I E R R E! WHO! " I asked, watching her as she fell. Linda's laughter was contagious I couldn't stop myself joining in the hilarity.

Linda had again been able to release all the tension in my body with the help of laughter. I am so lucky to have such a remarkable friend.
Putting it all behind me wasn't going to be easy, but I had to try for the sake of my sanity. Linda and I spent the rest of the night listening to the Beatles playing softly in the background, whilst planning our special holiday.

" The long, and winding road... "

But, we still hadn't decided where we wanted to go. It was a toss up between Butlin's Filey in Scarborough or Butlin's Bognor Regous. Organizing our precious holiday always made us feel important. We felt all grown up. We were in control. We were going to be two independent pals together. We would ponder over what clothes would take with us. How many pairs of shoes; bags;

dresses; and jackets the list was endless. At this rate we would need a removal van for all our gear.

Linda and I were going to be seventeen soon, and we were hoping our parents would allow us to go on holiday next year during the Glasgow Fair. When we would both be almost eighteen. But we still had to get to our mum's, and dad's approval. We would have to somehow convince them we were responsible adults.

This holiday, I'm certain, was going to be an experience we would never forget! I went home with a skip in my step. Happy with the knowledge that our holiday could be just another winter away...

CHAPTER 13

Meeting Francie And Josie

As the weeks passed my job continued to be great, and it was exciting meeting all the famous artistes. Everyone had to be measured for his or her outfits. Sylvia would do the fitting with the tape measure, and I would write down the sizes. It meant we were in the company of a lot of big named stars: Rickie Fulton: Jack Milroy: Una McLean and many, many more. Most of them I had never even heard off. It was fantastic because they were always such good fun to be around. I was so HAPPY! I really loved working at the King's.

As the months went by I was eventually allowed to make costumes from scratch, and Sylvia always made sure I received all the credit for my work. On one occasion Francie, and Josie came to collect their trousers, which I had been working on.

" Hullawrerr, china's, " they would echo as they walked into the room.

" Ah rare job yev done Sylvia, " Josie said with delight.

" Aye, it's a grand job yev done, SURE Josie! SURE Josie! " Francie agreed.

Sylvia was laughing at their antics, but quickly informed them that the work wasn't her doing, but was done by her new assistant Patsy.

" Och, Patsy, ye know that yer jist wan in a million, " they said in harmony.

" Thanks, " I said shyly.

I was totally embarrassed, and could feel my face burn, and turn different shades of red. I could see Sylvia in the background sniggering at me being thrust into such an uncomfortable situation. When they had left the room I let out a big sigh of relief.

" Och, Sylvia I wis fair affronted, " but I couldn't help giggling at my silly reaction.

" Ye did fine, and you deserved the compliment, " Sylvia said with pride.

I couldn't wait to get home to taunt mum about meeting Francie, and Josie. Mum being a big celebrity fanatic who knew all the theatre stars business; who they were married to; whom they were supposed to be having an affair with, she knew all the gossip.

So as you can imagine she was always eager to find out who was having a fitting, and she would try to squeeze as much information from me as she could. I loved keeping her in suspense, and leading her on a path to nowhere. I couldn't wait to tell her that I actually took the hems up on Francie and Josie's trousers knowing my mum would be green with envy, itching for the tiniest bit of news. When I arrived home that night she was in the living room watching the television.

" Ma ah spoke tae Francie and Josie the day, " I said as I walked into the room; full of myself.

" Yer kidding me on, " Mum said automatically switching the television off, and staring at me to see if she could tell if I was being serious or was winding her up.

" No Ah'm no kidding. They both thought I did a good job with their trousers. They said ah wes wan in a million, " I said with delight.

" Och! Can ye no get me an introduction or sumthing?? " She asked a bit annoyed at being left out.

" Naw ma, it goes against ma contract, I hev tae respect their confidentiality, " I said trying to sound a bit sorry for her, but stifling a chuckle behind her back.

" Aw, well if ye say so, " and she quickly scurried off into the kitchen to make the tea, her face twisted with jealousy.

At work, Sylvia was forever praising me on my progress, and my self-esteem soared. She even gave me a raise in my salary. I could hardly believe I was getting paid so much money for a job I loved. Don't get me wrong, we worked hard, and sometimes we had to work overtime, in order to be finished in time for a performance. But it was worth it.

During one of our long conversations at lunchtime, Sylvia revealed that she was never able to have any children. Although Sylvia, and her husband William both wanted children, and had been trying for a long time to start a family.

Sylvia explained that she did fall pregnant once, but unfortunately she had a miscarriage, and lost the baby at three months. I could see the sadness in her eyes as she relived the pain of her loss.

" It's just one o' these thing in life, that can't be helped, " Sylvia said softly in a slightly quivering voice.

" A'm really sorry Sylvia, "

I got up from my chair, and gave Sylvia a big hug. I wasn't sure if this was the right thing to do. But I need not have worried. Sylvia hugged me back. I could see the tears well up in her eyes.

" It's okay, it was a long, long time ago Patsy, " she whispered in my ear.

I felt utterly sorry for Sylvia; she would have made a wonderful mother. And I couldn't help comparing Sylvia to my mum, and thinking how cruel life can be. Mum, I'm sure would have been much happier without children. And here was Sylvia desperate for a baby, but unable to have any. Life just seems so UNFAIR!

I felt a strong bond growing between us, over the last few months. And I was anxious to get rid of the guilt that I felt for having deceived Sylvia. I decided, now was the time to come clean, and own up to lying at my interview about my granny teaching me how to sew.

" Sylvia, Aye... have sumthing tae confess, " I said in a low voice.

" Oh, Patsy what is it, " Sylvia suddenly looked at me with a worried expression on her face.

" Aye! Aye! A'm sorry, Ah lied tae ye aboot ma granny being able tae sew, she couldn'ae sew a hem on a pair o' curtains, never mind making a wedding dress for ma Aunty Joan, " I spoke in a very serious tone.

" Och is that aw. I knew you couldn't sew the minute you sat at the wrong side o' the sewing machine. You had me really worried there Patsy, ah thought you were going tae say you were pregnant. "

" WHIT! Din'nae be DAFT! " Utterly shocked at her reply.

" It didn't matter that you lied, all that mattered was your ability to learn, and I saw your determination, and I knew you were a capable candidate for the job, I went with my gut feeling, and believe me it has paid off. "

" But ye never said onything, " I said in earnest.

" There was nothing to say Patsy. Yer granny would have been proud of you as a human being. Sewing is not that important it's only a job, " Sylvia said softly'.

Sylvia's compassion was too much for me I broke down I couldn't hold back my tears any longer. Sylvia quickly came over to me, and gave me a big cuddle. I was sobbing on to her shoulder as she held me. Sylvia continued to hold me until I eventually I regained my composure.

" Hey, don't upset yourself, we all tell little white lies sometime. " Silvia said jokingly trying to cheer me up.

Slowly, I unveiled the whole sad story about Gordon, my life with my mum, and why I was so desperate to get a new job.

" Aw, Patsy, you should have told me all this long before now, instead of keeping it all bottled up inside your head. You know I feel like slapping yer mother, and that Gordon fellow should be reported, and charged with assault, " she was now obviously angry, and frustrated at the way I was treated by my mum, and Gordon.

" Aw, Sylvia! Aye... Aye... a'm so glad ye went we yer gut feeling, and gave me a chance, " I almost said I loved her; I was so caught up in the emotion of the confession.

" PATSY! REMEMBER YER WAN IN A MILLION!!! " Sylvia said with sincerity, and we both howled with laughter.

CHAPTER 14

Booked At Last

It was very quickly approaching the end of 1969, and the thought that we could be going on holiday at the beginning of the seventies decade was definitely going to be a thrilling experience for Linda and I. I'm sure It's going be the start of a new era for both of us.

Our parents were still not convinced that we were capable of being trusted as two responsible adults who could go on holiday by ourselves.

My dad wasn't that interested in the holiday, mum was really my only obstacle, and I tried my best to persuade her. But she wasn't too keen to let me go, until I managed to secure an offer of front row seats to see Francie, and Josie for mum, Kirk, Helen, and the boys. She remained undecided, playing hard to get, but I finally clinch the deal with a signed copy of a programme of the show dedicated to mum from Francie, and Josie plus meeting them both back stage after the show. How could she RESIST?

Linda, on the other hand did very well in her exams receiving top marks all A's, pleasing her mum and dad immensely, and as a reward for her hard work they were willing to grant her permission to go on holiday.

Having at last been given the go ahead for our holiday, now all we had to do was decide where we wanted to go. It was still between Filey and Bognor Regis. At long last, Filey in Scarborough had won the toss up.

Saturday, bright and early, we headed straight for the travel agents. We couldn't wait to put the final stamp on our dream holiday, and seal our departure date.

Booked at LAST! We were so excited; We were over the moon; We were on a high, and needed to celebrate.

And now that we were seventeen we were allowed a lot more freedom we had progressed from the old church hall to a real dance hall.

Our local dancing venue was the Marquee at Paisley Road Toll. The building was formerly the site of a Post Office, Carriage-Hires and Funeral Undertakers in the 1900's. In 1921, William Beresford Ingles, designer and former owner of the Beresford Hotel in Glasgow Sauchiehall Street, converted the building into the Imperial Picture Hall. It closed in 1959, and in the 1960's it became an Irish club. No alcohol was allowed on the premises so the punters had to either sneak it in or get drunk before they went. We preferred the latter.

Before the dancing we would drink some cider in Linda's house supposedly unknown to her mum and dad. It was, I know, a bit risky with Linda's dad being a policeman, but he never questioned us. He probably did hear the clink, clink of the cider bottles as we went up the stairs, and observed our clumsy departure from the house. I'm sure he was completely aware of our under age drinking, but chose to turn a blind eye.

We were always careful, and would hide the evidence, very discretely, in the bottom of Linda's wardrobe, until she could safely dispose of the glass bottles into the bin. Hopefully without anyone suspecting it was our empty bottles. It didn't take a lot of cider to make us tipsy. We were already drunk on the excitement of going on our first holiday together.

Once the cider had taken effect, we would set off for the dancing, singing as we walked to the venue. Making up our own words as we sang.

" We're going on a dreeee...m holiday
    Too... oo Butlin's in Fyl...eeee for a week or twoo... oo
    No more worries for me and you dum dum dum. "

Before we knew what hit us, we were standing outside the Marquee, still singing, and obvious to anyone watching that we were definitely under the influence of alcohol. It's a wonder the doormen let us into the dancing.

Of course we did get some funny looks from the bouncers, but they let us in anyway. I think one of them fancied Linda big time, and he was trying to get into her good books.

" Remember, I'll be here at the end o' the night if ye need a run up the road? " He said making serious eye contact with Linda.

" Aye, well I'll think aboot it, " Linda said keeping him sweet so we could get into the dance hall.

Once inside we made a quick dash to the toilets laughing hysterically at the antics of the bouncers.

The Marquee was a great location for Irish show bands, and the atmosphere was electric. It had a huge dance floor, and it also had this fantastic florescent lighting thing going on. I'm not sure how it worked, but when the lights made contact with your skin it turned it a deep brown. Everyone had a brilliant tan like you had just come back from a month in the south of Spain, and if you wore any white clothes the white became like a Persil advert. A brilliant white, hitting off your clothes, and making your tan look even darker. But unfortunately if you had dandruff, and wore black then it was there for all to see.

The high-pitched music sent everyone wild. But the highlight for us was at the end of the night when an Irish jig was played, and we would twirl, and twirl until we were dizzy. Sometimes the boys were a bit rough grabbing our arms, and swinging us around like rag dolls, but we were oblivious to any pain. We just accepted all the passion as part of the fun.

It was the next day when we looked at our aching arms, and saw all the black, and blue marks that we realised how much of a beating we had suffered. But we still didn't care; we had such a good time, it was worth all the pain.

We wouldn't have changed it for the world.

CHAPTER 15

Holiday Of A Lifetime

July 1970, and the day has finally come for our long awaited HOLIDAY OF A LIFETIME! Fred very kindly drove us to Buchanan Street bus station. Our bus was due to leave at eight o'clock in the morning. Linda and I didn't sleep much last night; the excitement of our trip had definitely disrupted our beauty sleep.

Everybody on our bus was going to the Butlin's camp at Filey. There was a fantastic atmosphere on board the bus, and everyone was obviously happy to be on holiday. Chatting to each other like old pals and passing sweets around, making the journey more enjoyable.

And it was wonderful feeling knowing we would be transported right into the camp. We were so excited on our first holiday together.

But it was no surprise to us when after about an hour of non-stop gossiping, that we were overcome by exhaustion, and no matter how hard we tried to fight it, we eventually had to give in we fell fast asleep. We didn't wake up until we reached the camp, when everyone on the bus cheered,

" We're here, WAKE UP!!! "

On arrival we all trotted into the reception hall, where the Red Coats gave a fantastic welcoming speech. Informing everyone about different events that would be available during our stay. We were also given a map of the camp to prevent us from getting lost. Having no sense of direction it was probably a good idea for us to carry the map everywhere we went. And perhaps this could prevent us from losing our way.

The Red Coats were a mixture of very attractive male, and females. Linda and I fancied almost all of the guys. Secretly I think we were both turned on by men in uniforms, but didn't like to admit it.

Our chalet was a bit on the small side, with two single beds squeezed together with very little space to move around. The bedroom was like an army barracks, bare walls, with dark blue blankets on our beds, and the same colour of curtains on our one small window letting very little light into our wee room.

On the up side it did have a separate toilet, and a sink, but unfortunately it has no shower or bath. Therefore that meant we would have to use the communal showers, which were a block away, but we didn't care. Nothing was going to spoil our fun. To us it was sheer luxury, a little palace to ourselves. It was a great feeling being miles away form home, and totally independent. Without having any interference from our parents. We were free at LAST!

Linda and I unpacked very quickly. We were eager to get out, and explore, and not waste a minute. Time was precious. We were flying above the clouds the sun was shining, and we were getting ready to hit the nightlife. It was only six o'clock, still plenty of time to wander around, and become accustomed to the layout of the camp, and also take a gander at what talent was on offer.

After drifting in, and out of the bars all night, we eventually found the disco. It was at the very end of the camp, situated on its own, away from the chalets, probably to stop the noise disturbing the campers.

We walked into the disco, and, to our delight the music was fantastic, and the talent also looked promising. It was now getting very late, but we still managed to get a couple of dances, and some drinks before it closed.

I spotted a very handsome guy standing at the bar, and as I looked at him he suddenly caught my eye, and smiled. He continued to hold my gaze for just a MOMENT...

But it felt as if we were the only two people in the entire room for what seemed like an eternity. The music, and the crowd faded into the background as if someone had turned down the sound, and all I could see was this guy at the bar smiling at me.

WOW! I had never experienced anything like it before. I thought I was going to pass out I felt as if all my blood had been drained from my body. I was completely struck dumb as I watched him leaving the bar, and walking out the door.

What was happening? It must be too much cider, and the travelling that has interfered with my brain cells.

" Linda, did ye see H I M?? " I asked struggling to speak.

" See who?? " Linda said wondering what was wrong with me.

" Ay've jist seen the love o' my life SMILE at me. Then walk oot the door, " I said still in shock, and with the adrenalin still rushing through my veins causing me to feel out of control of all my senses.

" Dinnae be so daft. Yer no yer sel. Too much excitement o' being on holiday his gon tae yer heed. Ye need a good nights sleep, " she said, instantly dismissing my feelings.

" Linda, ye might be right, ah dae feel funny, but no funny HA! HA! You never felt whit ah jist felt only a minute ago" I said, becoming a bit upset and annoyed that Linda wasn't taking me seriously, when I was trying to convince her, that I just had an amazing experienced.

But, I guess it was easier for Linda to think that I was overcome with tiredness, and had let my imagination get the better of me. Linda I know has never in her life experienced what I have just felt, therefore I can't blame her reaction, because I don't understand what actually happened myself. All I know is it felt so real, and yet so very unreal. Almost like a scene from a movie with me as the main character. I only hope it has a happy ending...

CHAPTER 16

Happy Smile Contest

The next day we got right into the spirit of the Butlin's camp atmosphere by taking part in one of the competitions. Linda and I entered the Happy Smile Contest. It was a hilarious experience.

We were supposed to smile, and expose our beautiful white teeth when the MC was asking us questions about our age or what part of the country we came from. But we were so embarrassed at being in front of an audience; we just couldn't stop giggling.

It was all taken in good humour, and even the audience laughed at our silly remarks. Linda did manage to win second place, but I wasn't even in the rating.

Linda was given free toothpaste, and a toothbrush. Plus she received some huge posters of tubes of red and white toothpaste, and a happy family all sitting in a row smiling with perfect white teeth, plus a certificate with her name on it. GREAT for brightening up the bare walls in our chalet. She is now a life member of the Colgate's ring of confidence club, minus the halo.

" Hey Linda, ah think ye were robbed ye shood hev wan. Ye've got the best smile in the whole o' Scotland, " I said slightly annoyed that Linda had only come second when she did have such lovely white teeth.

" NA! Patsy, yer biased. That girl hud straighter, and whiter teeth than me plus we're no in Scotland remember," Linda concluded.

Linda was right. I glanced over, and saw the girl standing only a few feet away smiling while she was getting her photo taken, and her teeth were not just brilliant white they were also perfectly straight.

We spent the rest of the day wandering around the camp, and I was glad we were having lots of fun. I didn't want to dwell on the previous night's apparition. I felt, I should let it pass, and put it down to a wonderful surreal experience. But secretly hoping I would bump into my Mr. RIGHT once again.

It was only our second night, and we were at the disco, dancing and singing our hearts out to the belting sound of " All right Now... " By a band called " Free ". When all of a sudden these two fellars tapped us on the shoulder, and asked us to dance. And as I turned round to face them I almost wet myself. It was HIM! The boy who had been standing at the bar the other night, and who somehow had the power to put me under some sort of hoo doo spell.

OH! GOD! Up close he's even more gorgeous. It still felt unreal, but I knew this time it was indisputable he was real, and standing right in front of me. Although I was completely sober, and fully aware of my surroundings I still couldn't understand the effect he had over me.

When the dance finished, he introduced himself. " I'm Steve, " he said. We chatted, and danced the rest of the night away. Linda danced with Steve's pal Pete, and they seemed to be doing okay.

Steve was very tall, and lanky, and had long brown shoulder length hair, and big brown doe eyes, and a smile that left me weak at the knees. If he had entered the " Happy Smile Contest " I'm certain he would have won. But then again I could be biased.

It was coming near to the end of the night, and the DJ started to play the last dance it was one of my favourite love songs " Will you love me tomorrow " by Carole King. It was the first slow dance of the evening, and the soft music instantly changed the atmosphere in the room

I hesitated, not knowing if Steve still wanted to dance, I turned away, and proceeded to walk off the floor. Steve gently caught my hand, and he led me into the most romantic last dance I have ever experience in my entire life. He held me tight, and it felt amazing being so close to him, and nervously I glanced into his eyes as we danced. I never wanted the dance to end.

So soon, and the night was over, Steve and Pete walked us to our chalet. We paired off on the way. Steve was keen to find out more about my family, my work, and me. He seemed to be absorbing every word I was saying, and storing it all up in his brain. I asked Steve, similar sort of questions, and I also kept every detail locked away in my head. We were standing outside the chalet constantly chatting away locked inside our own wee world.

After about half an hour Linda, explained she was tired, and said goodnight to Pete. Pete looked a bit disappointed that Linda had gone to bed so soon.

Disillusioned, and perhaps slightly embarrassed, he quickly disappeared towards his chalet. Leaving Steve and I on our own.

" Are you tired? Do you want to go? " Steve asked.

" No! No, I'm fine. "

" That's good, " and his happiness was evident in his smile.

Time seemed to disappear so quickly we were still standing outside talking, and we didn't even realise that the dawn was now breaking. One minute it was pitch black, and we were standing under a tiny light above the chalet door. Then suddenly the light went out, and at the same time the sun began to appear on the horizon causing a warm orange glow, and when it reflected onto the light blue sky all the colours merged together cascading into each other like ribbons of red, yellow, and orange. I had never in my life seen the sunrise, and by no means could I ever have imagined it would be so magical. It was incredible, and something I will never forget.

And at that very moment, Steve looked into my eyes, and he kissed me tenderly, and the warm feeling filled my whole body. I wanted it to last forever. Our first KISS! Oh GOD! I never felt anything like it before. Could this be love?

Reluctantly we said goodnight. But before Steve left we made arrangements to meet the next night. I was ecstatic. And so happy that he felt the same, and wanted to see me again.

When he left I went to bed, but I couldn't sleep. I was too keyed up. My mind was working overtime. I was replaying every little detail of events from the evening over, and over again in my head until I passed out. I'm certain I fell asleep with a smile on my face.

CHAPTER 17

Patsy (Cline) Stewart

The next morning Linda was already up, and dressed before me. I was still sleeping like a baby; I didn't even hear the noisy tannoy calling.

" GOOD MORNING CAMPERS. "

We were full board so it was a mad rush to get to the dining hall in time. I could easily have missed breakfast, but Linda wasn't having any of it, she dragged me out of bed, almost dressed me, and led me all the way to the canteen.

I really wasn't hungry I was still feeding on the night before. I couldn't wait to see Steve again. Over breakfast Linda and I talked about Pete, and Steve. I could tell Linda wasn't as excited as I was, but that's not to say she didn't like Pete. She just didn't seem to have any enthusiasm about meeting up with him again.

I was finding it incredibly difficult to contain my feelings, pretending to Linda that Steve really wasn't that important. Who was I kidding? I'm sure Linda saw right through my act. I was walking on air, and I never wanted to come back down to earth. It was the greatest feeling, and I wanted the experience to be everlasting.

After breakfast Linda and I decided to take a trip into Scarborough, and see the sights. It was a beautiful summer's day so we ventured on to the beach, and went for a swim. I found the warm water soothing, and I was having a fantastic time enjoying the glorious sunshine, but no matter what I was doing I couldn't get Steve out of my head.

Although Linda is always great company, I felt the time was still dragging on. I just couldn't wait to get back to the chalet, and start to get ready to meet Steve. But I didn't want to spoil Linda's day by rushing her back to camp I had to wait until she was ready to go.

Eventually we headed back, and sitting on the bus I could feel the excitement building up inside of me, and all I could think about was meeting Steve, nothing else mattered. I wanted to look stunning tonight. I wanted Steve to be knocked out when he saw me.

When we arrived back at the chalet I immediately started to get ready. Taking my time to get everything just right, I washed my hair with Voscene shampoo, which always made my hair really shiny. I put some rollers in to give my hair a bit of a curl, and a bounce. I made my eyes bigger by putting lots of mascara on. I wore my red mini dress, and red platform shoes. Linda took one look at me and stopped in her tracks.

" Wow! Patsy yer a stunner, " Linda said admiring my outfit.

" Thanks pal, I hope Steve thinks the same, " I said feeling a bit unsure.

" Be careful, remember yer on holiday, and holiday romances never work oot, " Linda lectured.

" I know. I know yer right, but I can't help it. I've never felt this way before, " I spoke without thinking, and didn't know why I wanted to cry, and shout for joy at the same time.

My feelings were all over the place. But it was a good feeling. Linda never said another word she just continued to have a worried look on her face. I felt guilty that she was so concerned, but what could I do. I was on a roller coaster, and I didn't want to get off.

We met Steve and Pete at the Beachcomber Bar. I could see Steve's smiling face as we approached. Judging by the look on his face I think he liked my dress.

We stayed in the bar all night until it closed. Linda, and Pete appeared to be getting on alright, but to be honest I was so engrossed in Steve's conversation, that I wouldn't have noticed an avalanche until it hit me in the face.

Steve and I were sitting very close together, cosy in our space. We were slowly getting to know more about each other's likes, and dislikes. And having lots of fun revealing some of our little secrets. Bringing down the barriers was helping us to bond. It was really strange, I had only met him forty-eights hours ago; but I felt I had known Steve all my life and that I could easily tell him anything.

We were exchanging our stories when suddenly I felt the mood alter, and I could see that Steve was struggling with his emotions. He slowly explained that his dad had died only a year ago, and I could see the deep sorrow in his eyes. I listened closely as he disclosed how distraught he felt, after his father died so suddenly. I felt privileged that Steve allowed me to have an insight into his pain. I gave his hand a slight squeeze, and kissed him softly on the cheek. Steve smiled, and kissed me on the lips. I wanted to change the mood, and cheer Steve up so I decided to reveal to him how my mum called all her sons after a famous Hollywood star.

" My oldest brother is named after Kirk Douglas, my middle brother is named after Dean Martin, and my youngest brother is called Fred Astaire. And none of them can sing, dance or act, " I said grinning.

" Oh Yeah, and who are you? " Steve asked.

" Guess? "

" Patsy, Patsy, Oh I don't know of any famous Patsy's. "

" Patsy CLINE! My mum's favourite country and western singer. "

"Oh, I've heard of her didn't she sing a song called Crazy."

He looked at me, and then he burst out laughing almost choking on his lager. Our laughter filled the bar. I almost cried with happiness seeing the pain leave his sad eyes, but I kept a tight hold of my emotions, I didn't want to spoil the moment with tears.
Too soon, and the night was coming to an end. We were all walking back to the chalet, and I started to panic. What if he didn't want to see me again? I began to walk more

slowly trying to make the night last longer. Soaking up every second, and wishing that it could be never ending. Savouring every minute of time spent in his company, and hoping Steve felt the same.

Then as we approached the chalet, Steve asked me if we could meet the following evening. I was thrilled, he still wanted to see me, but I didn't want to appear too eager.

" That would be okay, " I said deliberately trying to hide my excitement.

All four of us stood outside the chalet, but Linda said goodnight to Pete after only a few minutes. Pete didn't wait around; he excused himself, and proceeded to walk back to his chalet. Leaving Steve and I alone.

As soon as Pete was out of view Steve and I went wild, and kissed without stopping for a breath. I could hardly control the passion, which was flowing, through my veins. It was an incredible feeling.

Eventually we had to control our excitement, and we just held on to each other without a word being spoken relishing every second. Till finally we had to part, but saying goodnight was the last thing we wanted to do. But thank god, there was always TOMORROW!

CHAPTER 18

Falling In Love

Lying in bed I was thinking about all the things Steve had told me about his mum, and dad how they were the opposite to mine, encouraging their son to go to university, and supporting his decision to become a doctor. It must have been devastating for Steve losing his dad so unexpectedly to a massive heart attack. He was only forty-two.

His dad died last year, and his feeling for his dad is still very raw. I could see the hurt in his eyes. I felt truly honoured that Steve was willing to let me share in his grief.

Steve also has a younger sister called Anna, and she's only twelve. He told me he loves to tease her, and is always playing silly jokes on her. But since his dad died, Steve feels a great responsibility to his mum, and Anna.

Although Steve is twenty-one, almost four years older than me, I feel he is even more mature than your average twenty-one year old. Maybe losing someone you love forces you to grow up a lot faster.

He knows where he's going in life, and is totally focused on becoming a doctor. There were moments when we were talking that I felt inadequate compared to Steve, and that worried me greatly. I feared that I might not be clever enough for him or his family.

During the day Linda and I did our own thing, and I did enjoy her company, but if I were really honest I would rather have been with Steve. I felt that I couldn't breathe unless Steve was near me. Silly I KNOW!

Linda continued to lecture me on the reality of the situation. She knew I was, like her, still a virgin, and she worried that I might get carried away in the excitement of the holiday. Linda had never seen me so wrapped up in someone before. Little did she know I was just as WORRIED!

We all spent the rest of the two weeks together meeting every night spending our time at the disco, or in the pub. As we all became more familiar with each others habits, a lot of teasing went on followed by great gusts of laughter. I loved every second. And I was pleased that Linda, and Pete joined in the jokes, and I'm confident they had a good time to a certain degree, but it was obvious to us that there was no romance between them, and their relationship was purely platonic.

What a shame, because they did look good together, Pete is a very handsome guy, with long black hippy type hair hanging down his back, and the bluest eyes I have ever seen.

Linda never complained about meeting Pete every night. Although deep down I knew she would have preferred not to. I believe she was willing to make the sacrifice for me, only because she knew I really cared about Steve.

Linda and Pete's blessing allowed our romance to blossom, giving Steve and I the opportunity for our love to grow. Linda, totally understood my feelings, and I can't ever thank her enough. I will be forever in her debt.

Steve and I did feel a little guilty restricting our best friend's holiday, but after a lengthy discussion on the subject, we both came to the same conclusion. If the circumstances were reversed we would do exactly the same for them. We would without doubt also give up our time to allow our best friends the freedom to fall in love.

Every night after Linda, and Pete left us on our own we would walk down to the beach, and just sit almost glued together on a bench, and gaze at the waves cascading onto the sand. Shimmering white, and frothy until the water disappeared into the sand, and the waves would ebb away back to sea. It was so peaceful to sit there on our own and watch nature perform such a beautiful picture. And every night the light from moon glistened in the sky; it was so romantic I wished it could last for an eternity.

With each day that passed, was a day nearer to the end of our holiday. The clock was ticking fast, and I was completely aware that soon we would be running out of time, and our two weeks would soon be over.

Without a doubt I was disappointed that our holiday was coming to an end, and I was also dreading having to go back home without Steve. But most of all I was panicking at the prospect of saying goodbye to Steve. I wanted so much to still be able to see him every day.

When ultimately, the time does comes to leave the camp; I know it will be one of the most difficult things I have ever done, but I will have to find the strength somehow to let Steve go without any fuss.

And maybe one day in the future, if our love is our destiny, I'm confident we will meet again...

CHAPTER 19

Our Last Night Together

On our last night Linda and Pete suggested that we didn't all meet up as usual. Explaining he and Linda wanted some time on their own. But Steve and I knew it was just a ploy, and they really wanted to give Steve and I more time to be alone on our last evening together.

We never made any fuss or tried to change their minds we were simply grateful to them for allowing us the luxury of the extra time together on our own. I owe Linda BIG TIME!

Steve and I were going to the Steakhouse restaurant for a meal. He wore a bottle green suit, with a bright yellow shirt and a hanky to match. The hanky was sitting neatly in his breast pocket exposing a small piece. I must say he looked very distinguished. I put my red mini dress on knowing how much he liked it.

" Hey, ye look all posh? " I said pleased that he had made such a big effort for our last night together.

" Patsy, you look amazing. I'm glad you wore that dress. Red really suits you, " and he pulled me close, and kissed me.

We talked for hours, and hours about what we did as kids. The toys we had, the books we read, and what type of music we liked. We both loved the Beatles. I couldn't believe it Steve's favourite song was the same as mine "Hey Jude ".
Leaving the restaurant, and walking slowly back to the chalet we started to sing at the top of our voices, full of passion " Hey Jude " Absorbing every note, every step of the way.

" Na!, Na!, Na!, Na! Na! Na!, Na! Na! Na! " Laughing hysterically at the end of the song.

Although our hormones were definitely disturbed, and the excitement between us was way out of control, but still Steve never tried anything. And if I'm being honest, I really wanted him to take me back to his chalet, and make wild passionate love to me. But instead he was a perfect gentleman. Perhaps I should have teased him more, but I was too scared that I wouldn't be able to handle the consequences if I lead him on.
We walked down to our special bench near the beach, and sat there silently. He kissed me tenderly, and held me very tight as if he didn't ever want to let me go. Steve said he wished we didn't live so far away, and I agreed. It was comforting knowing he felt the same.

When I put my head on Steve's shoulder, and I buried my face into his dark green jacket, I could smell his scent, and I knew at that moment that if I never saw Steve again I would always remember his fragrance for the rest of my life.

I didn't want to cry, but my heart was heavy. I was coming down from the clouds with a huge thud. Why? Did it all have to END?

We exchanged addresses, and phone numbers. Steve seamed to be as enthusiastic as I was to continue our romance. And he reassured me that we would see each other again, and that Halifax wasn't the other end of the world only 200 miles away.

" Patsy, don't worry, once I learn how to drive there will be no stopping me, " he said never letting his eyes waver from my face.

" Och, ah know, I'll be all right, " I said trying to contain my feelings.

Reluctantly we walked back to the chalet, and Steve kissed me once more, I desperately wanted to say I LOVE YOU, but the words wouldn't come out of my mouth; I was terrified to revealed how I really felt in case it would scare him away.

I said I love you again, and again, inside my head, and I watched him as he slowly walked away. And the emptiness I felt when he was no longer in sight was overwhelming.

I gently crept into my room; Linda was already asleep. I had a massive lump stuck in my throat, and the ache in my heart was unbearable, and the only way I knew to relieve the pain was to cry out.

But I mustn't wake Linda up. I was so scared, I might disturb her, and I didn't want her to see the extent of my torment. She would be distraught if she saw me in such a state.

I very slowly tiptoed into the toilet, and softly closed the door, trying my best not to make a noise, hoping I wouldn't wake Linda; I was unable to contain my feelings any longer. I picked up a towel, and stuffed it into my mouth to help to muffle the sounds of my sobbing. But the pain was worse than I expected. I have never experienced anything like it before.

It's impossible to say how long I sat on the toilet. But even with the release of the tears, I was still in agony. I'm positive someone must have pierced my heart with a skewer the hurt was excruciating.

I eventually became too exhausted, and cold to stay in the toilet any longer. I forced my body to crawl into bed. I had no energy left to take my clothes off, and so kept them on. I curled up into a foetus position, and gained some comfort from the closeness of my limbs entwined together.

There were no tears left, and I had completely lost the ability to think. My mind was a total blank. I gladly collapsed into a coma.

CHAPTER 20

Kinks

In the morning, when I awoke, Linda must have seen my puffed up eyes, and that I was still wear my clothes from the night before. It was obvious I had been crying, but she chose not to ask any questions, and I was thankful that she said nothing.

On the long journey home I didn't talk much, and neither did Linda. I'm positive she felt I needed time to think. Sitting on my seat in the bus I closed my eyes, and slowly I tried to analyse my feelings for Steve, and I wondered at the magic of falling in love.

One thing I had clear in my mind was that I definitely would never forget him, and he would always have a place in my heart. And, I know, I'll be forever grateful to Linda for the part she played. She allowed me to see Steve every night without once complaining.

What a PAL!

When we arrived at Buchanan Street bus station the rain was chucking it down, and in a weird way I was glad it was raining. It reflected my horrible depressing mood. Fred was at the bus station waiting to take us home. Fred, was his usual chirpy self, which normally I found endearing, but because I was feeling so sad, Fred's cheeriness was irritating me so much that I felt like screaming at him. How could he be so jovial, didn't he know my heart had been shattered into a million pieces?

" Hi Girls, did ye hev a good time? " He said smiling as he put our cases in the car.

" Aye, it was great, " I said trying to sound cheerful, but obviously I wasn't convincing.

" Whit's up we your face? " Fred asked.

" Leave her alain, she's in love, " Linda explained.

" Is that aw? Not to worry ye'll get over it, " Fred teased.

" I know, I know, " I said struggling to reply.

" Hey, why dae ye no come oot we me the night? I'm doing ma roadie for the Kinks at the Barrowland tonight. It will be a free night. Whit dae ye say? " Fred asked optimistically.

" That would be great. Whit do ye think Linda? " I asked Linda making a half-hearted attempt to lift my mood.

" I'm up fir it. If you are, " replied Linda not convinced that I wanted to go.

" Aye, it would be great tae get oot, and forget aw ma worries, " I said.

Sitting in the front seat of the car I knew that I didn't really want to go. Normally I would have been ecstatic at the opportunity of seeing the Kinks. But I was finding it exceedingly difficult to raise my spirits.

All I wanted to do was mope, and wallow in my gloomy state. Play my love songs, and meditate about my Steve. But on the other hand, it's not every night you get the chance to see a famous band; my love songs can wait. And, I am indebted to Linda; so therefore going out is probably the best option, and the right thing to do considering Linda's sacrifice during our holiday.

Linda and I have been to the Barrowland many times, but we have never seen a top band like the Kinks. It is bound to be an amazing night. When I arrived home with Fred, mum and dad were out. I quickly got ready whilst Fred waited. I left a note for them explaining I had gone to the Barrowland with Fred.

We were all allowed into the dance hall early before any of the fans arrived, so Fred, and the rest of the roadies could set up the equipment ready for the group.

Linda and I were sitting not far from the stage watching Fred, and the other guys working, when we saw Ray Davis approach the stage. It was evident that he was checking out their work. I saw Fred talking to him, and Ray glance across at us.

Then to my surprise Ray Davis started walking over to where we were sitting. I never thought for one second, he was actually coming over to talk to Linda and I.

Linda and I had jumped out of our seats to greet him, but we stood there speechless like two waxwork dummies from Madame Trousseaus.

" I believe your Fred's sister " Ray Davis asked as he shook my hand, and then he smiled.

" Hope you enjoy the show. Any requests? " He said now shaking Linda's hand, and grinning at our hopeless response.

Linda stood there with her jaw sitting on her chest, but not a sound came out of her mouth. And I must have swallowed my tongue, because I also was unable to facilitate speech. We never answered his question. We just stood there tongue-tied.
Then in a flash, he was gone. In all the years I've known Linda I have never seen her stuck for words until NOW! Miraculously as Ray Davis walked away our voices returned.

" WOW! PINCH ME; PINCH ME; PATSY! I must be dreaming, " Linda screamed.

" Naw yer no, Linda its fir real, " I said ignoring her plea
.
" Ah thought ah wis gonnae pass oot, " Linda said the colour coming slowly back into her cheeks.

" Aye, well ye didnae, but whit a claim tae fame pal, a KISS from Ray Davis, " I said keeping my face straight, and stifling a grin.

" Hey, wait a wee minute, did ah miss sumthing, did ah black oot? " Linda said a bit confused.

" Naw ye didnae, but did yer granny no teach ye how tae suck eggs, " I said grinning.

Linda took one look at my face, she saw the devilment in my eyes, and instantaneously we both burst out laughing. We were fully aware we had shared a special moment.
What a brilliant night. The Kinks were absolutely fabulous, and we had a fantastic time. Dancing, and singing along to all their songs. And then to our delight half way through the concert Ray dedicated one of the Kinks songs to us.

" I'm singing " Sunny Afternoon " for Patsy and Linda. I heard it's one of your favourite songs, " he said.

We were gob smacked, but delighted that he took the time to dedicate a song to us.
At the end of the evening Fred drove us home, and his poor ears had to suffer our singing all the Kinks songs. We could barely remember the words, but that didn't stop us. No! Linda and I sang at the top of our voices, and we belted them out over, and over again until we were hoarse.
Once in the house, I collapsed into my bed far too exhausted to think about Steve.

CHAPTER 21

Leaving Patsy Behind

Pete and I were home by midday. Travelling up on the train Pete sat quietly in his seat reading his newspaper, allowing me the time to wallow in my dejected mood. Pete saw my sad expression, and realised that I must be really struggling with leaving Patsy behind, and he was giving me the space that I needed to come to terms with the separation.

Saying goodbye to Patsy was even more difficult than I could have ever imagined. It felt like part of my body had been chopped off, and I didn't feel a complete human being anymore. I wanted to hold on to Patsy forever.

I'll never forget as long as I live the way she looked into my eyes, as if she were examining every fibre of my sole. Her greeny blue eyes will be fixed in my memory for all eternity.

" Pete, tell me again why I had to leave Pasty behind? " I asked sounding confused.

" Patsy has to go HOME! To her family just as you have to go HOME! To yours, " Pete replied sounding a bit bored with my love life.

" I know. I know Pete. It's just that I've never felt this way before, " I said almost starting an argument with my best mate.

" Hey. I've never seen you like this before, but get a GRIP man you're phoning her tomorrow. It's not the end of the world. She's only gone to Scotland, not bloody well AUSTRALIA, " Pete said sounding a bit pissed off with me.

Steve's mum Christine was at home pacing the floor waiting for her son to arrive. Christine is tall, and thin with an elegant look. Her glossy brown hair set immaculately in a Jackie Onasis style flick. She looks good for her forty years, but sadly she's unable to hide the sorrow in her deep blue eyes.
Impatiently walking up and down the hall, Christine was now looking out the window; she kept her eyes peeled to the street, until the taxi drew up, immediately she ran outside. Waiting impatiently on the pavement as Steve got out of the cab, and instantly hugging her son close, not wanting to let go, and forgetting for a fleeting moment that he was no longer a baby. She quickly composed herself, and walked back into the house.

" How was your holiday son? " She asked as Steve threw his case down in the hallway.

" Oh, mum it was the best. I met this fantastic girl called Patsy, " I said eager to reveal all the particulars of the holiday.

Mum, and I are very close, and I wanted her to be a part of my happiness. I described Patsy, carefully, in detail, to do her justice. I emphasised that not only was she the most gorgeous person to look at, but she was also gorgeous inside as well. It was extremely important to me that mum understood completely what an amazing person Patsy is, and why she is so special to me.

Initially, after dad died, the only reason I kept on studying, and appearing to function was for mum, and Anna. I could never let them down. I couldn't let them see the full extent of my pain, and I hid my distress deep inside of me not wanting them to see my profound grief. I knew how much they depended on me, and I had to be strong to help them come to terms with their tragic loss. I am positive that mum, and Anna were fearful that I might drop out of university, and give up my dream to become a doctor. Although, I continued to reassure them that I was fine not wanting them to have an added burden of worrying about me. But when I was alone, and away from mum, and Anna's scrutiny, I was in fact a broken man.

Difficult as it was, I persisted with my studying, but now, not only for mum, and Anna, no I realised I needed to succeed, and attain my goal for DAD. I knew how proud he would have been when I qualified, and I had to keep going knowing it was dad's dream for me to become a doctor. Losing dad left a void I thought I would never be able to fill, but meeting Patsy has changed my life.

When I am with Patsy I am able to express my feelings allowing me to let go of my profound sorrow. Patsy has saved me, and to think I didn't even want to go on holiday. Mum, Pete, and Anna pressurised me into going.

" Steve, I'm so so happy for you, I've been worried about you. Since your dad died I know you have struggled, and I know the shock has been traumatic. But it looks like you could be turning a corner now, " mum said smiling softly.

" I'm fine mum, don't worry, " I reassured her.

" STEVE! STEVE! Your back! I've missed you, " Anna shouted loudly as she ran down the stairs two at a time.

Anna is tall for her years, and very skinny with long brown soft curly hair, and big brown bambi eyes like our dad's. Anna had just turned twelve, but for the first five years of her life I was nasty to her. I felt she had invaded my space, and had taken all my parent's attention. I was jealous, and didn't want to share my mum, and dad with a baby that was forever crying.
But after a sudden scare of meningitis, when I thought she might die, I felt really guilty, and had even convinced myself that it was all my fault she had become so ill. That scare changed how I felt about Anna, and I must confess after she recovered I kept a watchful eye over her, making sure she was always safe.

" Hey, Its good to see you I've missed you too, " I said as I threw her up in the air forgetting for a second how big she has become, and almost dropping her.

" Did you have a good time? " Anna asked eager for news about the holiday.

" Yeah, it was the best. "

" Did you, em, get me anything? " Anna said with a shy smile on her face.

" Oh no, I forgot! " I said pretending just to annoy her.

" Not to worry, " she said trying not to care, but with a disappointed look written all over her face.

" Would Scarborough rock, and a bracelet do? "

" FAB! Steve, just FAB! " Anna said jumping up and down smiling, and hugging me at the same time.

What a girl!

Although I was missing Patsy terribly, I was still glad to be HOME!

CHAPTER 22

Dad's Outburst

I never saw mum or dad when I arrived home on the Saturday. I missed them, in the mad rush to get ready for the Kinks gig. It was late Sunday morning, and I was sitting at the kitchen table eating my Cornflakes, when I first came into contact with mum.

I had brought mum a momento back from Scarborough, a large dark blue, and white marbled coloured glass type ornament of a fish with the words Filey written on it. I don't think it was to her liking, because the expression on her face was one of disgust. But not to worry, I thought it was lovely.

" Thanks, hen, but whit is it? "

" It's a fish, " I said indignantly.

" Aw, is it. Well ah suppose it could go in the bathroom?"

" Ah thought it would be nice on the bathroom windee sill, " I said quite pleased with my choice of present.

Mum swiftly proceeded to sit down beside me at the table, and began to ask me some questions about the holiday. I explained that Linda and I had a great time. And at first I hesitated to mention Steve, but swiftly changed my mind to see what her reaction would be. I didn't however, elaborate on how serious our romance is.

Mum's interest amplified, and she was almost interrogating me about Steve's background, where did he live; what did he work at; what did his mum, and dad do for a living; did he have any sisters and brothers? I answered all her queries, and emphasised the death of Steve's dad at such a young age, hoping she would feel some sympathy, and warmth towards his family.

She didn't seem to have any compassion for Steve's father's death. No, her main interest was focused on what happened between Steve, and me while we were together. I answered all her questions reassuring her that nothing underhand went on. But she gave me no feedback; she could have at least made some sort of comment good or bad. Nor did she even bother to declare that she had missed me, or was now; glad I was back home.

Why do I care so much? Why am I telling HER! ANYTHING! About my life?

Acting as if I wasn't hurt at her response, and hiding my true feelings, I casually informed her that Steve and I were going to keep in contact, by writing the occasional letter. And pretending to be nonchalant I quickly mentioned, that Steve would be phoning me tonight around six.

Dad had his usual thunder face on. He went about his business in the kitchen, and never asked a dickey bird about the holiday. He was rambling on under his breath something about blasted studs for his shirt. Busy moving plates, lifting cups, looking inside any nic nacs on the shelves hoping to find at least one precious stud.

I interrupted his concentration and handed him his wee present, he never even made eye contact with me.

" Whits, this? " He grunted.

" Open it an see, " I said encouragingly, but I already knew what his reaction would be.

" A key ring, what am ah going dae we that, whit a waste o' money, " and he threw it on the table.

I was a bit upset at their reaction. Not even a cuddle for their only daughter just returned from her first holiday away from home. But I guess it was only to be expected nothing had CHANGED!

Me going away for the first time in my life for two weeks wasn't a long enough break to transform the habits of a lifetime. They obviously didn't miss me.

Anyway, I didn't care what they thought anymore, Steve was phoning me tonight, and I was ecstatic. I couldn't WAIT! Five minutes to six, and I was pacing up, and down the hall. Six o'clock on the dot, and the phone rang. Good! He's on time.

I never really appreciated the phone before, but now I was so glad that mum and dad had decided to put one in the house. It was for me, now the most important piece of technology ever invented.

I picked up the receiver. It felt so good to hear Steve's voice. We very quickly got deep into conversation, and I was amazed at how easy, and natural the banter went. I was totally relaxed, and happy talking to Steve. I described the scene with the Kinks, and how Ray Davis came over, and shook our hands.

" Would ye believe Linda wis struck dumb? " I said laughing down the phone.

Steve also laughed at my description of Linda standing with her mouth open. " That's a first for Linda, " he said. We chatted away. Losing all concept of time, but blissfully contented to be listening to each other's voice. Then suddenly our world was interrupted. My dad yelled at the top of his voice.

" Git aff the f****** phone, " he bawled.

It was obvious that Steve must have heard my dad, his voice was so loud, and I'm convinced the whole south side of Glasgow must have heard him as well. I felt humiliated, and shocked. I didn't exactly know what to say next. I panicked, and somehow I was able to utter some words before putting the phone down.

" I better go, " I stuttered before putting down the phone.

I don't remember saying goodbye. I wanted to throw the phone at dad. I sat there seething with rage. AND at that moment I suddenly had no fear for this ignorant man.

"DA! Da! WHY! Did ye gee me, such a showing-up, " I said crying with frustration, and anger.

" Don't ye tell me whit tae dae, I'm yer faither, and ye need tae show me some f****** respect. "

He was now up close to me only an inch between us, and spitting in my face with his ugly temper. I quickly came to my senses and didn't continue to argue with him. I was now trembling with fear and really scared that he might hit me.

What a welcome home. I ran to my room. Tears pouring down my cheeks. Disgusted with my dad for interfering. He's destroyed my life. What am I going to do? I curled myself up into a ball, and cried myself to sleep.

I must have eventually fallen into a deep sleep, because I woke up with a START. Ring… ring… ring… my alarm clock was RINGING!

I must have slept straight through the night. But I was shocked, and upset to discover I had slept so long without any intervention from mum.

Where was the motherly love that I craved so much, she didn't even take the time to find out if I needed her. What kind of a mother is SHE!

I quickly got out of bed I still had all my clothes on. I glanced in the mirror. What a shocking sight I looked dreadful my eyes were all red, and puffed-up, but I had to go to work. I couldn't let Sylvia down. I washed, and changed my clothes, and to be honest I was pleased I was going to work. I needed to get out of the house. I didn't want to be under the same roof as mum or dad.

By the time I arrived at the King's my thoughts were more constructive. I had decided I would write a letter to Steve, and apologise for my dad's behaviour. I only hope he will understand.

It was so good to see Sylvia's cheery face. Her smile lifted my mood immediately.

" Well then, how was your holiday? " Sylvia asked, anxious for news.

" The Holiday was unbelievable... " I said. But remembering how happy I was on holiday filled me with sadness. I couldn't speak. I was completely overcome with emotion, and couldn't stop the tears.

" Oh Patsy, What has happened to make you so miserable? " Sylvia was now cradling me in her arms as she spoke.

Now sobbing uncontrollably. Slowly, I regained my composure, and bit-by-bit I revealed the details of the holiday. I tried to describe the magical moment I met Steve, and the way he made me feel the first time I saw him. But I could never recapture that instant for someone else. It's something you have to live through to truly appreciate the experience.

Then I went on to explain the horrible details of Sunday night. When my dad was shouting, and swearing at me whilst I was on the phone talking to Steve.

" I hung up the phone without saying goodbye. Sylvia I was in such a state, and I'm positive Steve could hear every word dad said. I was MORTIIFIED! "

I was still finding it difficult to come to terms with the situation, and unable to stop the tears as I recalled the terrible incident.

" Patsy. Listen if Steve really cares about you, and it sounds from what you've told me that he does, your dad being an ass won't put Steve off. I'm POSITIVE! Believe me. Don't upset yourself. Write your letter, and explain the circumstances, " she said softly holding my hands in hers.

Sylvia was right. Steve would understand that the situation was out of my control. I'm in no doubt now after discussing the situation with Sylvia. I'll write a letter tonight and apologise for my dad's bad behaviour. Thank GOD! I have someone like Sylvia in my life.
Sylvia had once confided in me, her one regret in life was that she didn't have a family.
What a TRAGEDY! That someone so sweet wasn't able to have a baby, because she is a natural mother, a very loving, and caring person.
I wonder if she would ever want to adopt

CHAPTER 23

A Phone Call To Patsy

Sunday I lazed around in my room listening to the radio, reading the papers, and trying to keep myself occupied waiting patiently until it was time to phone Patsy. I just couldn't get her out of my head.

At five minutes to six I was pacing the floor in the hall staring at my watch willing the time to go faster. Six o'clock at last I picked up the phone, and dialled Patsy's number, I was a bit nervous, I hesitated, and took a deep breath. What IF? Patsy had changed her mind, and had now decided not to keep in contact after all.

I was positive I was being silly, and over reacting, but I couldn't help it. I didn't want to lose her. I nervously listened to the ring tone drumming in my ear, beads of sweat running down my brow. Then the ringing stopped, and I could hear Patsy's sweet voice come down the line. I knew in an instance when I heard her speak, that she was pleased I had called.

" Hi Steve, its great to hear your voice, " Patsy said.

" Same here, I can't believe we are talking, and that I left you less than forty eight hours ago, it's amazing. "

Patsy and I were talking for what seemed like only seconds, when all of a sudden I heard a lot of shouting, and swearing in the background. I guessed it must be her dad, but before I had the chance to calm Patsy in her predicament the phone went dead. Shocked, and bewildered at the sudden outburst, and Patsy's hasty departure. I was left feeling helpless, and dejected wondering what on earth I could do now to help the situation?

My first instincts were to call back, and tell her it was okay, and not to worry, but I didn't want to aggravate the problem, and make matters worse for her. She had previously confided in me about her dad's bad temper, and how he was always shouting at her for the slightest little thing.

I sat glued to my seat in the hall with the receiver still in my hand, reflecting on what had just transpired, I was confused, and angry, but I knew I had to calm down. I needed to think this thing through with a clear head. I don't know how long I was sitting there, but eventually I came to the conclusion that it would be much better for Patsy if I waited until she contacted me. What an abrupt end to a beautiful conversation between two people in love.

Mum walked into the hall, and saw me staring into space.

" What's wrong son? You look like you've just lost a million pounds, and you were so happy before you went

on the phone. Oh, no! Patsy's not dumped you already...
Has she??? " Mum asked tenderly.

" Mum you won't believe this, but while I was talking to
Patsy, her dad was shouting, and swearing at her to get
off the phone. He sounded like a maniac, " I explained still
reeling from the shock.

" You were on the phone for more than an hour son,
maybe he was waiting on an important call, or had to
phone someone, " mum said trying her best to find an
explanation to why Patsy's dad would react in such an
ignorant manner.

" Mum, I don't imagine for one minute that he was
waiting for a call, Patsy, has told me he is a very selfish
man, and all that he can think about is going to the pub
with his mates, and having a bucket full, " I said my voice
reaching a high pitch tone I was now very angry again,
and frustrated at the whole business

" Calm down Steve, it sounds like Patsy knows how to
handle the situation, " mum replied trying to defuse my
anger.

" Do you think I should phone back? "

" No, give Patsy's dad time to cool down. You don't want
to aggravate the situation, and cause her anymore
trouble, leave it for a day or two. "

" Okay, if you're sure, " I said uncertain of what was the
right thing to do.

" Listen son, I don't want to sound negative, but you are both very young, and 200 miles may not seem a lot, but in a relationship it could be the one thing that drives you apart, " mum looked worried, and quite sad.

" Mum how can you say that. You were only eighteen when you got married, and dad was only nineteen, and you were both happy until... " I said defensively, but not wanting to cause mum any more grief by talking about dad. But it was too late my mum was clearly upset, and almost in tears. And it was all Patsy's dads fault, I hate the man.

" I don't regret for one minute marrying your dad, but we lived in the same street. We saw each other every day. I loved your dad from the age of ten when he tied my shoelace on the way to school. But if he had lived in another part of the country I'm not sure if our love would have survived. I'm not saying give up, I'm only trying to warn you not to raise your hopes too high, because I don't want to see you getting hurt. "

" I won't mum, I promise please don't look so worried. This is the best thing I've felt for a long, long time, " I gave mum a hug, and she let out a big weary sigh.

Lying in bed that night I was still unsure about how I was going to deal with the situation. Part of me wanted to write a letter straight away, and the other part Mr. Sensible, didn't want to make matters more difficult for Patsy. I decided to be Mr. Sensible, and give her some time to think. I only hope Patsy still wants to continue, and doesn't let her dad scare her into ending our relationship.

All day Monday I kept myself busy preparing work for going back to university not wanting to dwell on the possibility, that our romance was over. Patsy might have been bullied by her obnoxious dad to finish all correspondence with me. I hope I'm wrong. I'm sure I have nothing to worry about, and that Patsy is capable of dealing with her dad's outbursts.

The weather was sunny, and so later that afternoon I decided to catch up with some of my mates to play some football. Pete was there, and he couldn't wait to tell all the lads about our holiday. And of course he had to mention Patsy. Typical, Pete had to make himself out to be a martyr.

" Well guys, I have to tell you about our fantastic holiday, I had to spend every night with Steve, Patsy, and Patsy's pal Linda. It was torture. No excess drinking. Not even a different babe every night. Oh NO! Just Linda, and Patsy," Pete was wallowing in his tale of woe.

" It wasn't that bad...was IT! " I asked.

" NO, No I'm only joking, " Pete, laughed.

" I'll make it up to you one day. "

Pete ignored me, and shouted. " Steve's in LUUVE, " and all the guys laughed.

" So WHAT? You're just jealous, " I said trying to defend my image.

And then they all shouted out in chorus.

" Who LOVES YA?? BABY!! " I couldn't help myself I ended up laughing with them.

I could see the funny side, none of my friends had a serious relationship, and to be honest I never really wanted one either. But now that it's happened I wouldn't change it.

I owe Pete big time for agreeing to go out with Linda when he didn't find her attractive. And I am totally aware that Pete would have rather been out on the town with me every night drinking, and partying all the time. Plus meeting lots of different girls.

But he was no angel of mercy; he never made it easy for me. There was a constant nagging session, and a lecture every night from Pete before we went out. What do you say we hit the bars tonight? Or what's so special about Patsy anyway? A couple of times he over stepped the mark, and we nearly came to blows.

He did, however, have a get out clause. If he saw someone that he really liked he wasn't obliged to continue going out with Linda. Lucky for me there weren't any Bridget Bardow's in the camp, or else he would have been off like a shot.

CHAPTER 24

Patsy Apologised

After another restless night sleep I was happy to get out of my bed early, and put an end to the constant churning bad dream of never seeing Patsy again. It was Tuesday only two days after that horrible phone call. I was sitting in the kitchen drinking my coffee, and patiently waiting for the postman.

Hoping that Patsy would at least send me a letter, and put me out of my misery. I heard the letters drop to the floor. I ran into the hall, eager to find out if there was one for me. I quickly siphoned through the mail, and I instantly recognized my name on one of the letters. My heart was now racing, as I ripped the letter open. It was from Patsy.

I apprehensively read the letter, my main thoughts, and concern was that Patsy, would be bullied by her detestable dad, into finishing our relationship. But, I was wrong, the letter was an apology from Patsy for her dad's shocking behaviour, but more importantly she wanted to continue with our relationship.

Good for HER! She was stronger than I gave her credit. She wasn't going to allow her dad to come between us. What a RELIEF!

Patsy came up with a plan, which would allow us to continue phoning without her dad's knowledge. Her idea was a simple one, but could be a bit tricky; she wanted me to phone her at a set time when her dad was out, but there was just one problem with that arrangement, I might not always be available to phone at that particular time.

So I suggested instead that Patsy could phone me, when her dad was safely out of the house, and take a chance to see if I was at home. I could possibly miss some of her calls, but if that's the only option we have then we will have to try to make it work.

It was clear from Patsy's letter that she was worried that I was the one who wanted to end our romance. Good god! If she only knew what I was going through these last two days, waiting desperate for some news. She would I'm sure, be more confident that our relationship was strong enough to withstand, her dad's crazy outburst.

Although, I still didn't have a clue what was going to happen in the future, I did know I wanted to stick with it. To give up after the first little hiccup would have been an easy choice. I can't dismiss my feelings, I'm sure I love Patsy with all my heart. Ending our relationship would be far too much of a sacrifice.

I was still scrutinizing Patsy's letter when mum walked into the kitchen.

" Oh! Good morning son, you're up early? " Mum was a little startled when she saw me in the kitchen.

" I couldn't sleep. "

" Well, judging by your face, and the letter you're holding, it looks like you'll sleep tonight? "   Mum said smiling.

" It's from Patsy, we've found a solution to fix our problems, " my enthusiasm was obvious. I was thrilled that Patsy was willing to persist with our romance.

" I'm pleased for you, and I actually DO hope it works out for you. "

" Thanks mum, I really need your support. "

" You know son, you'll always have that, no matter what."

I left mum in the kitchen mulling over her coffee, and went up to my room. Sitting at my desk I wrote a long loving letter reassuring Patsy, and strongly expressing my feelings. Explaining that there was no need for any apology, it wasn't her fault, and I strongly emphasized that she wasn't to blame herself. I reinforced my love to Patsy, stating that I would not, under any circumstances, let her dad break us up. We would, however have to be patient, and everything I'm sure will work out in time.
I made it clear to Patsy that I was sorry I had not been there for her, but if I had enough money, or could drive I would have jumped into my car, and been up to see her in a flash. But, for now it was important that she knew that in the future I would take a train or a bus, and be there to

give her a great big hug, and kiss. I would somehow find the money to comfort her in her hour of need.

Money had been tight since dad died, and I had no spare cash. I had a Saturday job in a grocery store, which helped finance my holiday, and allowed me nights out with my mates, but I totally depended on mum to get me through university.

After I posted my letter I lay on the top of the bed regurgitating what mum had said the other night, and wondering if maybe she was right, and the distance is going to be a bigger problem than I anticipated.

Although I was beginning to have some very slight reservations about the 200 miles distance between us, being maybe more of a problem than I first thought. I was however, in no doubt about my feeling for Patsy. I have to push these uncertainties out of my mind, and become more focused on my love for Patsy.

And I'm certain we will eventually get through this, and that love will PREVAIL...

CHAPTER 25

A Letter From Steve

Impatiently I waited all week for Steve to reply to my letter. Although I was extremely busy at work preparing for this years pantomime " Babes In The Wood ". Rushing from client to client, having to be a hundred percent accurate in fitting their costumes.

But still the days dragged on, and the nights were a combination of sheer panic at the thought of losing Steve, followed by utter elation when I became calm for a minute, and I realised I was over reacting.

My mind was like a helter-skelter; I couldn't get Steve out of my head. I was desperate for an answer. Hoping he hadn't given up on our relationship.

Finally a letter arrived on the Thursday morning. Thank god! I read it quickly. Then I read it yet again. But this time slowly lingering over the words: miss you: can't wait to see you once more: and lots of love, and kisses Steve.

Steve assured me not to worry about my dad. But to avoid upsetting him at all costs, he suggested we should try to be especially careful, and be more organised. Maybe you should wait until you're absolutely certain he's gone out, and won't be back for a few hours, before you attempt to phone Steve advised. This was a far more sensible idea. I always knew he was a clever laddie.

At work the following day I was on a high, I was up in the clouds dreaming of seeing Steve's face, and kissing his lips. Sylvia knew the moment she saw me walk in the room, that I had obviously received good news.

" I take it by the look on your face, lover boy has sent you a letter, and the romance is back on," Sylvia asked grinning like a Cheshire cat.

" Aye, Steve sent me a lovely letter, and he still wants us tae continue writing, and fir me tae phone him. But preferably when ma dad is oot, " I said smiling.

" Well what did I tell you? You had nothing to worry about. "

" Aye ye were right, "

I ran over to Sylvia dragging her from her seat, and forcing her to dance to the sound of "Dancing in the Street... " Playing on the radio, and with me singing along.

Sylvia simply joined in the singing, and dancing hilarity with ease, and I could sense that she was really happy for me. I felt so fortunate to have someone like Sylvia in my life. It's ironic, but in some respects Gordon did me a big, big favour. I now have so much more love in my life here with Sylvia. I feel blessed.

When I got home from work that night dad was out. Great I could phone Steve before dad gets back. But I better check first to see if he has just popped out for a paper, or if he is out for the night.

" Ma, where's dad? "

" He's away tae his pals hoose tae watch the fitba. "

" Is it awright if ah phone Steve? "

" Remember whit yer faither said. Ye better no be on fir lang, " mum emphasized.

She still hasn't even acknowledged the fact that dad had been ignorant, and wrong to bawl at me the other night when I was on the phone. I don't think she even cares?

" Aw right ma, I'll watch ma time, " I said obediently.

The phone rang out for a couple of minutes, and it was Steve's mum who eventually answered the call.

" Is that you Patsy, Steve's told me so much about you? "

" Oh! Oh! That's nice, " I said apprehensively.

" I'm glad I've had the chance to say hello, I'll go, and fetch Steve, I won't be a minute, " she put the phone down, and I could hear her shouting on Steve in the background.

I was a bit nervous talking to Steve's mum for the first time, but she sounded so sweet, and genuinely pleased to be talking to me that my anxiety left me very quickly. Steve came to the phone, and again nothing else mattered, but the fact that we were locked in conversation.

We talked, and talked, we were encapsulated in our own wee bubble. Once more, the time disappeared, and before we knew where we were it was time to say goodbye. I put the phone down, and went into the living room. Still savouring Steve's voice in my head. Mum was sitting on the couch. She gave me a funny look as I walked into the room.

" Ye really like him. Don't ye, " mum asked with a disgruntled tone in her voice.

" Aye, ah dae, " I said in my defence, and wishing Steve was beside me.

" Aye well, whit a shame he lives so FAR away, " but there was no sadness in her tone. And I'm sure I could detect a bit of delight in her statement.

" Aye, it IS! " I said raising my voice up a pitch.

She shrugged her shoulders, and turned her back away from me, continuing to watch Coronation Street. I was left standing in the middle of the sitting room suddenly feeling totally alone in her presence. I could detect a strong feeling of disapproval in her manner, but could not understand why she was acting so coldly.

Why was she not happy for me? Was she jealous? I sat down on the couch contemplating whether I should reveal how I really felt about Steve. But the longer I sat there with the television blaring in my ears, the more I was certain it would be better not to say anything. She was more interested in Elsie bloody Tanner's relationship to Len Fairclough, than in her own daughter's life.

CHAPTER 26

Linda's New Boyfriend

Saturday was still for me the best day of the week. Linda and I did our typical wonder around the shops. Today I was on a crest of a wave wondering around the shops, happy to be in love. Smiling at anyone that looked in my direction. I must have looked a bit dolly dimpled. But who cared?

When the shopping excursion was over, it was straight into the Blue Lagoon for our customary fish supper. Linda was desperate to read the letter from Steve, which I had never stopped harping on about, all morning.

While we were sitting waiting for out order I let Linda read the letter from Steve.

" W E L L? WELL?? " I asked impatiently waiting on her comments.

" I'm sorry tae say this Patsy, but ah think the boy has got it BAD! " She said after fully analysing my letter, and now with her elbows on the table holding her head in her hands, and staring into my face with a cheeky smirk.

" Dae ye really think so? " loving her reaction.

" Aye! Ah told ye Steve would get in touch, and wouldn't be put off by yer dad, " she said handing me the letter back.

" Aye ye were right again, as usual. "

" Well ah could say ah told ye so. "

" But seriously, dae ye really think we'll last? " Wanting a bit more reassurance.

" Aye, he's daft on ye, and fine ye know it, " Linda replied now with an exasperated look on her face.

" Och yer jist saying that tae make me feel good, " I acknowledged half-heartedly still acting as if it wasn't significant, but I was exceedingly eager to hear Linda's version on my love life.

" Naw I'm no, ah'm positive he really cares aboot ye, " Linda argued.

Of course, I was thrilled that Linda thought Steve was serious about me, but I was now well aware of the obstacles that could affect a long distance romance. We were just at the starting line, and Steve and I still had a lot of hurdles to get over.

Although I could have talked about Steve for hours, and hours I really didn't want to hog the conversation all day. So I quickly changed the subject, and asked Linda what was happening at university.

" Well, I've been getting chatted up by a guy in ma class " Linda revealed.

" Hey, that's great, and dae ye like him? " I asked.

" Aye, but he's no Paul Newman mind ye. But he his got sumthing, " Linda said enthusiastically.

" Och who wants Paul Newman anyway, Whits his name?"

" It's John "

" Ah that's a nice strong name, whits his second name? "

" Ummm; noo dinnae laugh, PROMISE me? " Linda starring at me with her big brown eyes almost bursting out of their sockets.

" Aye, okay, ah promise, ah promise, " wondering what on earth his name could be whilst taking a sip of coke.

" It's John Peel, " Linda whispered not wanting anyone to hear, and waiting attentively on my reaction.

Instantaneously, I burst out laughing, and spat all my coke over the table, coughing and choking on the rest that I had just swallowed. I grabbed a napkin to mop up the mess I glanced at Linda; her face was red with embarrassment. But she couldn't hold on to her emotions for long, and she ended up joining in the laughter.

I tried to contain myself, and deliberately didn't ask the question or sing the song " dae ye ken John Peel? " Although I'm sure she heard me muttering it under my breath.

" Hey, whits aw the commotion aboot? " Margaret asked as she helped to mop up the coke that had spilled all over the table.

" It's nothing, now don't ye say a word Patsy PLEASE! " Linda threatened.

" Och, a' Linda goan let me into the joke a', " Margaret pleaded.

" It's no that funny, believe me, " Linda insisted.

" Aw well a' if ye don't a' want tae tell me, " Margaret said a bit miffed.

" Oh, aw right then, I've got a new boyfriend, and his name is John Peel, " Linda replied with a sense of pride in her voice.

" Is that aw, I wance went oot we a wee fella called William Wallace, fae the Gallogate, and he wisnae called Wee Willie fir a' nothing, " she said, and at the same time she winked her eye.

" HA! HA! HA! " The laughter reached a crescendo, and filtered through the café. The tears were running from our eyes. We almost fell off our seats bent over with

bursts of laughter. Margaret had also joined in the hilarity, and was struggling to control her hearty laugh.
When Margaret had composed herself, and went back to her work. I waited until the hysteria had died down before I began to quiz Linda some more about her new guy.

" Has he asked ye oot yet? " I asked getting a bit more serious.

" Aye he his, but he wants tae go oot on a Saturday night."

" Well, whits wrang we that? " I replied.

" But, WE! always go oot on a Saturday. "

" Never mind aboot me if ye like him go fir it. "

" Are ye sure Patsy? "

" Aye, nay bother. "

Linda looked happy, and I was pleased, she had met someone special. It was funny in an odd sort of way not having the holiday to chat about any more. When I think about the countless hours we had spent arranging, and rearranging our plans for our dream holiday, and now, it's all in the past. Sometimes I still can't believe we've actually been away for two weeks. It disappeared so quickly.
But for me it was more than a holiday. It was a life changing experience, and I can't explain why, but I feel

that Linda and I are now on a different path, and about to begin another chapter in our lives.

On the way home we made plans to go to the Marquee. And once inside the dance hall we never left the floor the entire night. Linda and I went through every routine in our repertoire, and we had an amazing time. We were young, and in love.

The last dance was the usual Irish jig, and we swung each other around, and around until we were dizzy, accidentally letting go of each other's hands, and ending up falling on the floor in fits of laughter. What a NIGHT!

I think we both knew, life was now going to be different for us in the future, and our time together would be limited. We walked up the road, our arms linked and chanting at the top of our voices. We were both in love, and we wanted the world and his wife to know.

We sang, " My Guy, " in harmony with great passion, and gusto completely convinced that our guys were the BEST!

We were oblivious to the noise that came out of our mouths; we knew we were never going to be in the same league as Mary Wells. But we didn't care. Then before we knew it we were home.

Blissfully happy, but tired, and ready to go to bed and DREAM...

CHAPTER 27

CHRISTMAS 1970

I can't believe it's Christmas 1970, and that Steve and I are still writing to each other. Steve sent me a huge Christmas card with the words I love you written in big letters, and a pair of red woollen gloves, and a wee white hanky with my initials on it. I will treasure them forever.

I sent Steve a black crew neck jumper, made from Shetland wool one of the latest fashion items for men. Everything seems to be going great, we are writing two letters a week, and sometimes if I'm lucky, when dad's out at the pub, I manage to squeeze in a couple of phone calls.

I know people were doubtful and thought that it would never last a month, even Linda I'm sure had her suspicions. Well we've proved them all wrong, we are still as eager as the first night we met, and it's nearly six months gone. And over the last few months we have even started to plan a holiday together for the summer, when

Steve finishes his exams. And it's almost similar to when Linda and I were planning our holiday last year. It's become the highlight of our conversation, and I'm certain it's going to keep our romance alive until we are able to see each other once again.

Linda and I still meet up on Saturdays, and that's when we catch up on all the hot gossip, and have a good blether. It's a great pity we didn't manage to see each other more during the week, but Linda is usually caught up with her studying, and she needs to spend time with the now love of her life, John. I don't mind because I'm also busy working overtime for the forth-coming Christmas panto, and most of my free time now, is spent writing letters, and singing along to my music.

With all the time I spend singing along to my records you would think I was now able to at least sing in tune. Not so, however I can belt out a song with commitment to the lyrics, but I know deep down I'll never be as good as Cilla, Lulu, or even my namesake Patsy Cline.

Cilla's ballad " You're my world, you're every breath I take... " Is a great love song, and makes me aware of how I really feel about Steve every minute of the day. Lately, I appear to be constantly humming this song unconsciously. I can't seem to get it out of my head.

I don't really miss going out to the dancing on Saturday nights with Linda, but I do miss Linda's banter, and her incredible sense of humour. She can be a great tonic, when you're feeling down. But, we are now aware that our time spent together is very precious to both of us. It's our quality time.

I'm happy being busy at work it helps me to stay focused on the costumes, and stops my mind daydreaming about Steve. If it isn't a panto then it's another Stanley Baxter show. But I don't care; it won't be long now until the summer holidays.

I was cosy in my little world wishing the cold winter away, and planning our future holiday. It didn't matter where Steve and I went as long as we were together. I just know it will be fantastic when we meet again. I can't WAIT!

Then out of the blue, for the first time in six months, I never received a letter on the Tuesday. I thought that's okay there's no need to panic. I knew Steve was studying for his forthcoming exams, and would be pressed for time. I was a bit disappointed, but I understood the pressure he was under.

Saturday came, and there was still no letter. I remained calm, but a little bit concerned that something might have happened to Steve. No panic, I will phone him tonight when I get back from the town. Glasgow was packed with shoppers for the January sales, and it wasn't much fun being constantly pushed, and shoved to the side all the time. Linda and I decided to give up on chasing the bargains, and instead headed straight for the Blue Lagoon earlier than our normal time. We just had to get away from all the hecklers.

I had phoned Linda during the week, so she was aware that Steve had not written. And she was her usual positive self.

" Patsy, stop pitting yer sel through hoops. I know it's no easy, but I'm sure Steve's jist been too busy with his exams. That's aw! " She said with conviction.

" Yer right Linda, I'll phone him tonight, and find oot if onythings wrang. "

I decided to change the subject away from Steve. I had a bit of a juicy scandal to share with Linda, and I was dying to tell her the news.

" Did ah tell ye, ah bumped into Jean fae the office? " I asked.

" Naw, ye didnae, and fine ye know it, " Linda her eyes wide with interest.

" Well, ah met her in the queue outside the King's. She wis we her pal, " I said in a slightly soft slow tone lingering on every word.

" AND? AND? " Linda knew I was holding back on the information, and she was desperate to find out more.

" Aye, apparently, ye'll never believe this, " I whispered.

" GET! On we it, " she gave me a nudge.

" Well: ye remember WILMA! We aw that red HAIR! Well! Ye'll never believe it BUT! SHE! Wis having an affair we Gordon, she wis meeting him secretly at his flat every lunchtime. And what dae ye think? "

" WHIT? " Linda said almost hyperventilating.

" POOR! LAURA! Caught them in the act, " I was relishing every word of the story.

" Yer joking? " Linda now breathing normally started to giggle.

I could hardly contain myself, and burst into laughter. We were both almost falling off our seats with huge belly laughs. It was exhilarating.

" And dae ye think that's why Wilma gave ye that horrible look? " Linda asked tears of laughter running down her face.

" Aye, ah forgot aboot that, she was obviously jealous, and she must hev thought that ah, fancied GORDON! If she only knew the truth, " I started laughing again at the mere suggestion of me being even remotely attracted to Gordon.

" Did Laura end the relationship? "

" Aye, she did, and apparently Laura has now married Gordon's best pal. "

" Good for her. Ah telt ye he wid get his day, " Linda said with huge satisfaction written all over her face.

" Aye ye did, but poor Wilma, she lost her job, " I said feeling a bit sorry for Wilma.

" Well that's whit happens when ye play we fire. "

" Aye yer right, I gave Jean ma phone number, she said that she wanted to keep in touch. "

On the way home I began to get a bit excited at the prospect of phoning Steve. I had to be certain that he was well, and had not been sick or involved in a nasty accident.

CHAPTER 28

ANOTHER BARNEY

When I arrived back home from Glasgow. Mum, and dad were having one of their arguments. They didn't even hear me come into the flat. Dad was bawling at mum, and blaming her for losing his studs for his shirts AGAIN!
But mum was holding her ground, but adding fuel to the fire by telling him it was up to him to look after them.

" Why dae ye no pit them awa where ye'll find them, " mum raged.

" Whit! That's your job, " sliver spitting out of dad's mouth, and splashing onto mum's face.

" Stop yer spitting, yer nothing but an allki, " she said wiping her face with a hanky.

Dad took one look at mum, and then at me. I could see the steam coming out of his ears. He grabbed his black scarf to hide his bare neck, and walked out the door BANGING! It shut as he left. Almost taking it off the hinges.

GOOD! I can phone Steve now. I was aware mum was watching, but not realizing there would be a problem. I picked up the phone, and was about to dial Steve's number when mum screamed at me.

" Whit are ye daying, pit that phone doon, " mum shouted obviously still angry.

" I wis jist gonnae phone Steve, mum. If that's aw right? " I said a bit shocked at her strong reaction. Usually she never seems to mind if I used the phone.

" Naw its no awright. I'm gonnae use it tae speak tae yer Aunty Joan, " and she proceeded to grabbed the receiver out of my hand.

Mum obviously wasn't in a happy mood. Therefore, there was no point in me upsetting her anymore. I could phone Steve tomorrow, or maybe he will phone me tonight, there was no rush. No need to panic. I quickly made myself scarce, and went to my room to listen to some music.

Tomorrow mum was planning to have Sunday dinner for Kirk, Helen and the boys. Which meant dad would have to be on his best behaviour. Kirk wouldn't stand for any of dad's nonsense. And dad knows he would have to watch his mouth when Kirk was around.

It was around one o'clock when they all arrived. Dad was in the living room nursing his hangover, and keeping out of mum's way.

Helen and I set the table for dinner, in the kitchen, we had a reasonably big recess where we had a gate leg table, which could be easily opened up into a large dining table. The seven of us could quite comfortably sit around the table.

Whilst I helped mum prepare the vegetables, Helen embarked on her favourite hobby, talking. And I knew before she even opened her mouth what she was about to say.

" Hev ye heard fae Steve yet. Yer ma wis telling me ye never got a letter recently, " she paused, and I grabbed my chance to try to change the conversation.

" Och, its early days, and he's sitting exams the noo, " I said trying to sound up beat.

" Is that so, well a'm sure ye'll hear fae him soon enough. Becoming a doctor canny be easy, he must be a clever laddie. You stick we him, and bla...bla...bla... " Helen continues to rattle on and on.

But I switched off. I was in no mood to listen to Helen blabbing on and on. Then to my surprise mum butted in, and saved me from any more torture. It's not like her to give me a helping hand.

" Helen leave Patsy alain, and go an tell the boys their teas oot, " mum insisted.

Helen looked a bit shocked at the sudden interruption to her flow of questions, but immediately obeyed mum's command.

The boys were all keen football fans, and the conversation around the table was dominated by how well Scotland was doing. And although no one could agree on how skilful Scotland were playing at the moment, at least everyone was convinced that the team being picked by their manager Tommy Docherty were the perfect players for their next match against England. Even dad approved.

I could see that the boys were really enjoying all the banter discussing the Scotland team, and for once we had a Sunday dinner without any fighting. In actual fact it turned out to be a very pleasant meal.

After dinner, I took Michael and Paul out sledging in the park, but after only a short time we ended up falling off our home made sledges, and then it was straight into a snowball fight where the two of them ganged up, and nearly killed me.

We had an exhilarating time. All the exertion left me totally exhausted, but it was just what I needed a complete distraction from Steve.

When everyone had left, and while dad had his wee after dinner boozy snooze subsequent to him drinking far too much beer. I was going to take a chance, and sneak a phone call to Steve. But mum was quick to warn me not to use the phone in case he woke up.

" Ah dinnae want any mair aggro fae yer faither. So keep aff the phone, " mum said glaring at me.

I felt a bit sorry for her. She looked tired and worn out after her fight with dad the other night. And the last thing she needed was for me to upset dad again. Mum was probably right it would be best if I didn't use the phone tonight.

I will go out and get her a wee sweetie from the shop on the corner, and I can call Steve from the public phone box; which was only minutes from the shop.

There was a big queue inside the newsagents, and I was becoming increasingly inpatient waiting to be served, I was desperate to get some change to call Steve. I could see the call box from inside the store, and it was empty at the moment, I needed to be dealt with quickly.

At last! I was served. Armed with my sweets, and lots of coins I headed straight for the phone box. I picked up the receiver, and dialled the number; I had my money in my hand ready. GOOD! It's ringing. It rang, and rang, but there was no answer. Oh, NO! There's no one at home. WHAT now?

I went back into the shop, and wasted some time gazing at the magazines on display. I was taking my time browsing, hoping when I phoned Steve back that maybe at least his mum would be at home, and she would be able to give me an explanation into why Steve hasn't contacted me. I'm certain I would know by the tone in her voice if she was hiding the truth, I don't think she would lie to me.

I was now getting some odd looks from the shopkeeper I got the feeling that he might be thinking I am about to steal something. Feeling uneasy, I quickly handed him the Jackie magazine with a story about Twiggy, one of my favourite models. He was still looking at me suspiciously, but he said nothing. But I could feel his eyes follow me as I left his shop.

I again headed quickly towards the phone box I dialled the number; and waited with irritation birr... birr... birr... still there was no answer. I banged the phone down angry at not getting a connection, and frustrated at having to leave the call for another time as a queue was now forming outside the phone box. BLAST! I will have to wait until tomorrow.

I hurried up the road the snow was falling heavily, and it was also beginning to get dark. I ran up the stairs, anxious to get in out of the cold. Mum was in the sitting room watching an old black and white movie with the sound blaring; she was trying to drown out dad's snoring. He was still on the couch sleeping. I gave mum the chocolate, and she seemed to be pleased with my gesture.

" Whit took ye so long? " She asked as I handed her the sweets.

" I tried tae phone Steve, at the call box, but their wis no one at home, " I explained.

" Oh, well then ye best leave it the noo yer dad's sure tae waken up any minute noo, " mum said, her eyes totally focused on the television.

" Aye, ye might be right. "

I went to my room put my pyjamas on, and jumped into bed all cosy, and with my favourite comfort food at hand; Fry's cream, and a Mars bar. For a brief time I was in heaven slowly devouring my chocolate bars. The sugar overload putting me on a high for at least ten minutes, then it was very quickly back to reality.

I started to read the article about Twiggy. Apparently Twiggy at the tender age of twenty had decided she didn't want to be a model anymore.

" You can't be a clothes hanger for your entire life, "

Twiggy had told reporters. Good for her, I'm sure she could do whatever she wanted to be successful. She is so beautiful.

I read my horoscope, which was interesting.

"Venus is looking after your heart strings, and there is nothing to worry about at present. You will soon be with the man of your dreams and it's only a matter of time until you are together.
Mars is offering his energy to get you through the rest of the month, and financial rewards could be yours. This is your moment. " If ONLY!

I read a few more articles, and then fell asleep.
My last thought before I drifted into the night was OH! How I WISH! I could talk to Steve right NOW...

CHAPTER 29

Waiting In Anticipation

All the Pantomimes were finished for the season, and work had slackened off. There were only bits and pieces to sort out for the next show. I desperately needed to be busy. I needed to stop my mind wandering, and worrying about Steve. I was really hoping we would be run off our feet, giving me no time to think, or dwell on my current crisis.

It was also unfortunate that Sylvia had taken a much-deserved day off. I know I was being selfish, but I couldn't help myself. If only Sylvia were here right now, I could off load all my problems. And I know she would do her utmost to help me put everything into perspective, and keep me sane. Oh! How I need Sylvia!

I couldn't contact Linda either she was knee deep into her studying for her exams and I didn't want to disturb her, I couldn't let myself be so selfish. No, I would just have to learn to be patient.

But all this free time was allowing my brain to run on all cylinders. Letting my thoughts run riot. Instead of being positive I was being negative. I was anxious to get home, and hopefully find a letter, which I know will put an end to my torment. But it was going to be a long, slow day.

At LAST! I was on the bus heading home. I ran up the stairs two at a time. I opened the front door, and shouted.

" MA! Ma! It's me, wis there a letter fir me, " I shouted before I had even closed the door.

" Naw, nothing, " she called back from the kitchen in her usual uninterested tone.

My heart sank to the floor. I was so disappointed. I can't go on like this I need to know one way or the other what's happening. I'm simply going insane with the suspense.

Mum was still in the kitchen, and I checked to see if dad was OUT! He was nowhere to be found. GOOD! I will take a chance, and phone Steve.

I picked up the phone, and dialled Steve's number. I was almost hyperventilating waiting on the phone connecting. Praying dad wouldn't walk in. DAM! DAM! It was engaged. Well at least someone was in I'll try again later. My mood immediately lifted at the thought of talking to Steve later.

" Patsy, yer teas oot. "

" COMING. "

After tea I went out into the hall to call Steve, but mum was on the phone. She's never on the phone long. So I decided to watch some TV whilst I was waiting. Steptoe and Son was on, Albert the dad was up to his usual tricks trying to interfere into his son's love life. It was just getting interesting, but then I heard the front door open. OH! GOD! I'm out of luck dad's was back. I could hear the shouting from the living room.

 " Are ye on that f******* phone again It's costing me a f****** fortune, " he bawled at mum.

 " Dinnae be say ignorant, I'm talking tae yer son, " mum shouted.

They were at it again. I would never be able to use the phone tonight. Maybe Steve will phone me instead. I need to think positive, and stop being such a drama queen. I'm sure I'll receive a letter tomorrow, and everything will be back to normal. I'll go and have a relaxing bath, and calm myself down.
The bath must have done the trick, I woke up the next morning totally refreshed, and with a different attitude I wasn't going to be silly anymore. I knew Steve loved me, and that couldn't change in a week. I had to have some faith in our relationship, and trust him to write back.
At work Sylvia was her usual bubbly self, and I was carried away with her good mood. I expressed my fears that I was really scared Steve had stopped writing for good. But I reassured Sylvia that after thinking it through sensibly last night I have now came to the conclusion Steve was probably caught up in his exams, and I'm sure there will be a letter waiting for me tonight.

" Steve's exams can't be easy, and I realize how important it is for him to do well not only for his mum, but for his dad as well. "

" That's the right attitude Patsy, you're beginning to mature, " Sylvia said looking at me with admiration.

" Ye mean I'm no a daft wee lassie anymore. "

" You were never a daft wee lassie, ye just needed to be shuved in the right direction, " she said grinning at me.

But, on my journey home sitting alone on the bus, I couldn't stop myself from thinking the worst. Although earlier in the day I had convinced myself that I wasn't going to panic anymore, and that I was NOT going to have any more negative thoughts.
But then my determination began to slip and my mind was weakening and I started to question myself.
What IF! He doesn't want to see me again!
What IF... It's OVER!
I didn't want to assume any longer. I needed to know? I jumped off the bus, and ran all the way home.

" MA, It's me, any letters fir me, " I shouted as I opened the door. I held my breath waiting on her reply.

" Naw, " she shouted.

That's it I've had enough. I walked into the kitchen, and threw my bag on the floor. I could feel the anger building up inside of me. I couldn't comprehend why Steve had still not bothered to send me a letter or even a little note.

" Whits wrang we ye? Yer face is like thunder, " mum asked.

" It's been over a week now, and Steve his nae answered ma letter, " I explained flustered with anger, and sadness.

" Din nae be so keen, a weeks nothing, gee him time. When yer studying fir exams the last thing ye need is some wan breathing doon yer neck looking fir attention. Gee him some space, " mum said with a determination in her voice I had never heard before.

Mum might be right; I need to calm down I will leave phoning Steve tonight I'll give him time, and take a step back to allow him to get through his exams. I won't distract him; it wouldn't be fair I do understand that it must be extremely difficult studying to become a doctor.
I spent the rest of the night reading the Jackie magazine in my room. An Agony Aunt column had a story about a holiday romance going sour. The girl was concerned her boyfriend, whom she thought loved her, had suddenly stopped writing. Her worry was has he found someone else?

" Yes! And only to be expected " was the brutal reply.

Holiday romances are like a fairy tale, and don't measure up to real life, the Agony Aunt went on to say.

That was all I needed to cheer me up. I should have bought the Bunty.
I could hear the phone ringing above my music. I lowered the volume on the record player. And I waited in anticipation hoping, and praying that it was Steve, and mum would call me. BUT nothing...
I continued to listen to my sad love songs. After listening repeatedly all night to Diana Ross, and the Supremes

singing, " You just keep me hanging on, " and unknowing
letting the lyrics interfere with my thoughts I couldn't
help wondering if Steve had NOW! Stopped, loving me,
and if I was just waiting around in vain?
Was he as the song suggests keeping me hanging on???

CHAPTER 30

Stilling Waiting

Two weeks have past, and still no letter. I desperately want to pick up the phone, and talk to Steve. But I'm now far too scared. I know if he told me on the phone that he had met someone else. I would be devastated, and I can't be sure how I would react. It would now be kinder to end the relationship in a letter, than to be told over the telephone. I wouldn't have to listen to his voice saying the words.

" I'm sorry Patsy, it's over I've found someone else, "

I couldn't bear to hear those words come out of his mouth. That is why I have to write one final letter with no pressure on Steve to continue our relationship. All I want to know is, are we finished, and why? Have you met someone else? Although it would break my heart I need to understand what has changed. I don't think I'm being mellow-dramatic now, I've given Steve plenty of time to get in touch, but he has failed to respond.

Dear Steve

Please can you take just a minute of your time to let me know if you've had a change of heart? Or if you have met someone else, I understand. And I wish you well.
But please, please don't keep me hanging on.

Write soon

Patsy.

I waited patiently all week hoping for an answer to my letter, but regrettably I didn't receive a reply. I can't BELIEVE! Steve has been so selfish, and he has rejected my plea once again.

WHY? Oh WHY! Hasn't Steve taken the time to answer my letter? I thought I knew HIM? And that he would at least do the decent thing, and explain to me what's gone wrong with our relationship, and not prolong my agony. Not knowing is unbearable.

Oh God, I just don't understand WHY? Steve is treating me in this way? I guess I was wrong, and he's not the wonderful guy I thought he was?

These last three weeks have been horrendous waiting every day for a letter, and none arriving. My heart is aching every waking minute, and I know it would be impossible to measure the amount of tears that has been shed in Steve's name.

BUT! Somehow, although it's been really difficult coming to terms with this heartbreaking situation, I have survived, and have managed to function. I don't know where I got my strength, because since I met Steve I had totally convinced myself that he would always be in my life, I never, for a moment anticipated an end.

What an IDIOT! I have been.

I am slowly forcing myself to come to terms with the hard facts. He doesn't want ME! Our holiday romance is now well, and truly over. And I have to let him GO!

I had convinced myself our love was strong enough to keep us going until our planned break in the summer. My expectations were I guess far too high. But, it is also incredibly painful to realize I was completely mistaken about Steve as a man.

I was in my room looking out my bedroom window studying the street below, and listening to the lyrics of the Beatles " Yesterday "...

Unable to stop the tears trickling down my cheeks, warm, and salty as they brushed my lips. I sat there staring blankly into space. I had no thoughts in my head, and no plans for the future, just an empty heart. Longing for that magic moment when we first met. " Yesterday... "

As much as I wish I could go back to yesterday I CANT! It's obvious that Steve has lost interest in what we had. And found a new love.

Tomorrow, Saturday I will be meeting up with Linda, she is unaware, that I still hadn't heard from Steve, and I'm dreading having to tell her. I KNOW! I should have contacted her sooner, but I have been too distraught to discuss my anguish, I couldn't let Linda see my suffering. It wouldn't be fair; she would be so hurt at seeing my pain.

My situation was now hopeless. My love life was DOOMED! And I knew it would be impossible for even Linda, to come up with a solution to save my relationship. On the bus into Glasgow I explained to Linda that I didn't fancy gallivanting around all the shops. I lied to her about my very busy week at work making me tired, and that I had a bit of a headache. Hiding the real reason deep inside my defeated heart. And, thank God for make-up.

" Are ye sure ye still want tae go tae the Lagoon then Patsy? "

" Aye, ah want tae get oot, it might clear my head. "

" Well if yer sure. "

I couldn't face looking at clothes, when I didn't have Steve in my life to admire my new outfits. I just wanted to have some quality time in the Blue Lagoon, and catch up with Linda's latest news, and hopefully take my mind as far away from Steve as I could.
Linda couldn't contain her excitement John was taking her away for a weekend to Blackpool; she never stopped talking about him the whole time we were on the bus. I must have given her the impression I was totally engrossed in every word she was saying, because she never halted, and to be fair, although my brain wasn't absorbing every word. The distraction was good for me, and it was great to see Linda so happy and confident in her relationship.

" OH! Patsy, ah think he's gonnae propose. "

" Aw Linda that's great, I'm so happy fir ye. " Linda was ecstatic and I was thrilled that she was happy.

Linda was absolutely over the moon at the prospect of John's proposal. She never paused for a breath until we were sitting in the Blue Lagoon, and I could then sense immediately what she was going to ask, before Linda even got the words out of her mouth. I only hope I can remain composed, and not breakdown. I don't want to spoil her thunder.

" Anyway, enough aboot me. Whits been happening we you and Steve? " Linda asked.

" Nothing, " I said avoiding her eyes.

" Why's that! Has he still no answered ony o'yer letters?"

" NAW! And ah sent Steve another letter at the beginning of the week, and I pleaded we him tae let me know where we stood, but there's still been nae reply, " my anger very evident, and stopping me from crying.

" Why dae ye no jist gee him a wee phone, and ye'll be able tae sort this oot, once an fir aw, " Linda said gently trying to coax me into making the call.

" Naw! Ah canny noo. A've lost aw ma confidence, " tears welling up, and I was finding it difficult to believe that I actually still had some tears left.

" Aw, Patsy ye let me blether on aboot John ye shood hev stopped me. Ah thought ye were waiting tae ye got tae the café before ye showed me yer letter. "

" Dinnae be daft, its good tae hear how well you and John are doing, and it will be great news if John proposes. Your company is the perfect medicine for me, " I said feeling a bit better at having shared my problems.

Linda was visibly upset, and she hugged me tightly against her I silently sobbed on her shoulder releasing some of the pain. She held me, and never uttered a word. Giving me time to recover.

" Hey, why dae ye no come oot we me, and John the night. John could bring one of his pals? " Linda was trying desperately to cheer me up.

" Na, I'm sorry but I'm no very good company the noo. "

" Och, ah wish ye never met Steve NOO, ye look so unhappy. "

" DON'T ever say that Linda; he's the best thing that ever happened tae me, and if it disnae work oot. Well I still don't regret one minute I spent with Steve, " and I meant every word.

" Ye know if ye ever need me, jist phone me, and I'll come roon tae yer hoose right away. "

" Ah, know that, thanks Linda. "

We spent the rest of the day chatting with the staff in the Blue Lagoon. Listening to all their love problems, and I watched Linda trying to be an agony Aunt. It was great fun; I even threw in my tuppence worth. It was just what I needed to take my mind off my own worries.
But I wasn't ready to disclose to any of the punters that my relationship was over. I was still emotionally unstable, and would need more time before I could talk freely about my lost love.

At home lying on my bed I reflected on the conversation I had with Linda. It hadn't been an easy task explaining to Linda that I thought Steve and I were finished. But telling her has helped me put things into reality, and it's pushing me forward, which is what I really need. I have to get on with my life.

I did appreciated Linda's concern, and was thankful for her support. I know if she could she would try to make things better for me, and take away my pain. But she CAN'T! NO ONE CAN!

Linda hasn't got a magic wand. But just knowing I'm not alone, and she's there if I need her, makes all the difference. I'm extremely fortunate to have a friend like Linda.

But even after all that's happened, I still would never have missed a second of, YESTERDAY...

CHAPTER 31

Steve's Given Up

" Steve! Three weeks is a LIFETIME! Come on out with the lads tonight, and have some fun? " Pete said getting exasperated with my constant refusal to go out with him.

" But, I just can't somehow conceive that Patsy would completely ignore all my letters. I thought she would at least acknowledge my plea to let me know if she wanted to end it, " I said still very, very angry at Patsy's lack of response to any of my letters.

" Forget HER! Your far too young to be serious anyway, " Pete emphasized.

" Your right Pete...But part of me just can't let go. I honestly feel like jumping on a bus down to Glasgow, and confronting her face to face, " my feelings were all over the place one minute, I was livid and I needed to

172

challenge Patsy, and the next I was worried that something serious had happened to Patsy.

" Don't be stupid MAN! Get over it! Come out tonight, and have a laugh like old times with your mates, " Pete encouraged.

" Okay! OKAY! I think I will come out, " I need a diversion, and going out could be the answer.

I was extremely annoyed that Patsy hadn't the decency to explain to me the reason why she had decided not to continue with our relationship. A short note would have been enough to put me out of my misery.
Dragging my feet I got ready, and went out with Pete. The bar was jumping, and the music was loud. Exactly the distraction I needed to help me forget Patsy, and maybe a crate or two of beer would also do the trick.
At the disco we met up with some of our old school mates, and were having a laugh. Some of the girls at the bar were teasing me, and one girl in particular Carol, was flirting with me more than the other girls. I must admit I was enjoying all the attention.
I remember having a big crush on Carol at school, but she always had a boyfriend in tow. She is a real beauty with big sky blue eyes, long blonde hair, and a body made in heaven. Her legs I'm sure go all the way to her waist. I never thought for one moment, she would even glance in my direction never mind want to talk to ME!
It was great Carol seamed happy to be dancing with me all night, and when I asked her if I could take her home, to my surprise she agreed. We got into the taxi, and before the cab had even moved away from the kerb, Carol was all over me. This girl wasn't shy.

Our first kiss, and she was already teasing me with her tongue. Her body was locked onto mine, and I could hardly catch my breath as the snogging continued, I didn't want her to stop. I was loving every second, and I just couldn't get enough.

Before I knew where I was the taxi had stopped outside her house. I went to get out, but Carol stopped me. She put her hand on my shoulder, and gently pushed me back into the cab. What a disappointment!

" It's okay, Steve, I'll be fine, here's my phone number. Give me a call if you want, " Carol said as she handed me her number on a piece of paper, and at the same time closing the door of the taxi.

" But! But! " I stuttered in shock.

'See yah! Bye, " she smiled as she waved goodbye.

" Umm, bye, " I managed to mutter.

I was a bit dazed at the sudden end to our passion in the back seat. Well Carol, definitely knew how to make an impression on a guy. I was hot to trot, but left gasping for more.

" Are you alright son? " The taxi driver asked with a grin on his face.

" Yeah, I'm fine, " I said with a big sigh.

When I got home I fell into a drunken sleep. I awoke about four in the morning choking for a drink of water. I sat up in bed drinking my water, and reflecting on the night before.

I was now deeply confused. What I felt for Patsy was so much different from what I felt for Carol last night.

I wanted to make love to Patsy the first time we kissed, but the feeling of love over took my feelings of lust. Respect kept me in control I was terrified to do anything to offend Patsy. I loved her so much. My heart still ached for her greeny blue eyes. Blast! I could still feel the anger build up inside me. I will have to be realistic, and face up to the fact that it's over.

Sex was high up on my agenda last night. I would have gone all the way if Carol had let me. Love, and lust can be one, but they can also be a world apart.

In future I think I will settle for lust. It's not as painful as love. I'm considering giving Carol a call later...

CHAPTER 32

Steve's New Girl

I fell back into a deep sleep, and didn't wake until midday. Mum was shouting from the bottom of the stairs.

" Steve, your lunch is ready. "

" Great, I'll be down in a minute, " I was feeling better, than I had felt in weeks.

Mum was already sitting at the kitchen table, she commented on how good I looked.

"Did something happen last night? You're looking happier than I've seen you for a long time, " she said smiling.

" Well, yes it did actually, I met a girl. "

" That's fantastic, I'm SO pleased for you. You deserve a break, " mum said giving me a big hug.

I knew mum has been worried about me these last few weeks, and she's been trying her hardest to guide me in the right direction. But I was being stubborn, and didn't want to listen to her; all I wanted to do was rush up to Glasgow, and look Patsy in the eye. And demand to know if she had found someone else. But mum insisted that I was crazy, and talked me out of going, suggesting that I should wait, and not make a complete fool of myself.
And! Unfortunately mum was right; if Patsy really cared she would have answered my letters. It's good to see the relief in mum's eyes when I said I had met someone else. I think I'll give Carol a call after breakfast.

" Hi Carol, It's Steve, " I said feeling a bit embarrassed remembering last night's heavy petting session in the back of the taxi.

" Hi, Steve, " Carol replied sounding pleased that I had phoned.

" I was wondering what your doing tonight? " I asked my confidence growing.

" Nothing special, Why? " Carol asked.

" I was thinking, if you would maybe like to go to the movies tonight? "

" Hey, that would be brilliant, what's on? "

" Kelly's Heroes," Donald Sutherland in it. Do you fancy going to see it?"

" Sounds good, I'll meet you outside the cinema at seven. Bye for now. "

When I put the phone down part of me was excited at meeting Carol, but I couldn't help feeling a tinge of guilt about Patsy. Although I know I did everything I possibly could to make it work. And I wrote endless letters practically begging Patsy to explain why she had stopped writing. BUT, still she chose not to reply.
I can't let her hurt me anymore. I have to get on with my life. She obviously has lied to me about her feelings, and although I wish it were different I have to move on. And Carol could be the one to mend my shattered heart.
I arrived at the theatre at five minutes to seven. Carol wasn't there, but I was happy to wait. She arrived only minutes after seven, and she looked great. She wore a blue mini dress almost the same colour as her eyes. And so very, very short revealing her fantastic legs.
Oh! NO I can't seem to divert my eyes from her legs.

" Hi, you look fantastic, " I said a bit surprised at myself for the sudden out-burst of compliments.

" Thanks Steve, " Carol said looking very cool, and collective.

Once in the cinema, I went to walk down the aisle when Carol grabbed my arm.

" Steve, lets stay at the back, " she said smiling.

" Okay. "

We had barely managed to get ourselves comfortable in our seats, when Carol started to kiss me. We were quickly wrapped up in each other's arms, and the passion was flowing way out of control; I could hardly catch my breath; she was all over me, and the excitement was exhilarating. I've never met anyone so over powering. She seemed to know what she wanted, and I only hope it's me. The picture had hardly begun when Carol whispered in my ear.

" Steve let's leave. "

" Are you sure? " I whispered back.

" Are YOU? " She said her eyes wide waiting for a reply.

" Lets go, " I said leading Carol out of the cinema fumbling our way along the row in the dark, standing on a few toes along the way. As we left we could hear lots of tuts, and moaning behind us.

Carol and I found it difficult to contain our laughter, and only managed to control our giggling until we reached the foyer. Then we were bent over holding our sides with tears running down our faces, and screaming with laughter.

Once outside we stood inside the bus shelter looking into each other's eyes reading each other thoughts. Then we went wild again, a bit over zealous. We couldn't get enough. Finally we stopped to catch our breath, but we knew we would be in big trouble if we continued to be so passionate in public view.

" My mum and dad are out tonight, and won't be back until late. Why don't you come back to my house? " Carol volunteered between the snogging.

" That's great, " I said a bit apprehensive, and excited all at the same time.

We jumped on the next available bus, and sat upstairs all cosy kissing, and cuddling at the back seat of the bus. We weren't on the bus for very long, which was just as well because Carol was teasing me again, and I was finding it very difficult to control myself.

Carol stayed in a big modern house not far from where I lived. We walked up the long driveway with trees at either side, and the lawn was massive, big enough for a tennis court. The grass was immaculately cut very short like a velvet green carpet.

Her front arched door was huge, with highly polished dark wood, and with big brass handles resembling the entrance to a church.

Once inside the house I was in awe of the plush surroundings. Cream shag pile carpets dominating the massive modern living room. And I'm sure most of the paintings on the walls were originals. I felt slightly inadequate in these affluent surroundings.

Carol was obviously aware that I felt uncomfortable in her home. She quickly offered me a seat on one of the big leather sofas, and she tried to distract my attention from such grandeur by offering me a drink.

" Would you like a drink? " Carol asked walking into the lounge.

" What do you have? " I asked casually as if I it was the norm for me to be alone in a big house with my girlfriend.

" Beer, vodka, gin, whisky, what ever your little heart desires, " she said brushing against me as she walked past over to the well stocked bar in the corner of the room.

" Beers fine, " I said, but suddenly I had second thoughts; thinking I may need something a bit stronger.

" Could I change that to a vodka, " I shouted in my suddenly very deep voice.

" Yep, no problem, " was her reply.

Carol sat down beside me on the couch her mood changed and she became a bit more serious. Carol explained that she didn't have any brothers or sisters, and that sometimes she felt a bit lonely in this big house. She wished that she had an older sister or brother to talk to, and share secrets.

Listening to Carol revealing her feelings on being an only child, I saw another side to her character. Although she likes to give the impression she is very much in control, I sensed when I studied Carol more closely that it's just a façade she portrays, and sometimes she's way out of her depth. But I get the feeling she will never admit her real fears to anyone.

Carol went back to the bar to refill my drink. Lying stretched out on the enormous black leather couch, I closed my eyes, and was thinking to myself this is the life. One day I would be able to afford my own pad with shag pile carpets, and gigantic leather sofa's.

" Hey, WAKEY! WAKEY! " Carol yelled into my ear as she handed me my drink.

" Sorry, I was just dreaming. "

" About what? " She said in a sexy voice.

" Oh, about you, and me of course, " I lied.

" Mmm; why don't we go upstairs to my room, and listen to some music? " Carol said seductively, and reached for my hands, pulling me up from the most comfortable seat that I have ever sat on in my entire life.

" Sounds good to me, " I said downing my drink in one gulp.

We walked up a grand staircase made in beautifully carved light oak wood, with huge mirrors on the wall with gold colour frames. What an entrance hall it was beautiful. Carol's bedroom was also very spacious, but it wasn't my taste, very girly, with lots of pinks, and flowers all over the place.
Carol went over to her record player, and put on a record. I could hear the familiar tune start to play.

" Will you love me tomorrow. "

Oh! No! I wish Carol had played another record, I had a flashback to Filey, and that first slow dance when I held Patsy in my arms. I wanted to run out of the house, I wanted to go to Glasgow. No! No! This is crazy I need to forget Patsy, and get on with my life.

Carol walked slowly towards me, not a word was said as she led me over to the other side of the room. She started to kiss me, and we fell onto the bed, our breathing becoming heavy with the increased excitement as we kissed. And as the music played softly in the background we made passionate love.

As we lay on the bed absorbing the memory of our passion. I didn't want to move, I was at last happy again with Carol lying naked across my bare chest I was in heaven, and it felt amazing.

What was that Scottish lassie's name again? Who cares?

CHAPTER 33

Let The Heartaches Begin

On Linda's weekend away John went down on one knee at the top of the Blackpool Tower, and asked Linda to marry him. It was a very romantic occasion with all the Blackpool lights shinning, and the snow flickering on the ground. Linda was ecstatic, and said yes instantly. I was so happy for her.

The snow has now gone, and the buds of spring are beginning to bloom. Life goes on as normal, everyone is going about his or her business as usual, and no one seems to really care that my heart has been broken.

I can't believe, three months have gone, and still not a word from Steve. My sad existence in my room remains static; I keep playing the same song repeatedly on my record player. " It's Over " by Roy Orbison, again and again! I know I'm a glutton for punishment. But I can't help it. I don't sing along anymore I just listen letting the lyrics beat me up.

I have to somehow let go. OH! GOD! But my heart won't let me. My mind is in a constant conflict with my heart. But the PAIN! Oh, god the PAIN!

My heart is silently weeping inside my body, and the tears are imprisoned; and can never ESCAPE!

I really wish I knew what to do to stop the AGONY!

BUT! I DON'T! I have to do something; I have to somehow, let GO! And get on with my life.

At work they've started a new young doorman called Frankie, he has been asking me out for months. He's a very good-looking guy. An Al Pachino look-a-like with the same jet-black hair, and ebony eyes. He is not very tall at five feet four, but his olive skin, and Italian good looks are striking features, which makes his height fade into the background. He has all the patter. But I'm convinced that he is a ladies man, and not to be trusted. He's the last thing I need in my life.

" Och, Patsy, jist come oot we me as a pal. Ye know, Ye want tae! " Frankie insists every time I pass him on my way into the theatre.

" Naw! Naw! Yer jist no ma type. "

" How dae ye know I'm no yer type, " he said.

" Ah can tell a mile away, yer no tae be trusted, " I said without looking at him.

" Ye know that's defamation oh ma character, withoot even a trial, ye know ah can sue ye, " he said trying to make his big eyes look sad as he held my gaze.

" Ye don't say, " I laughed at his feeble attempt to seduce me into feeling sorry for him, and maybe succumb to his suggestion.

Over the last few weeks Frankie has been very persistent, and I am getting a bit lonely playing the same songs over, and over. Perhaps it's time to come out of my room?
And now that Linda was engaged to John, it's only natural that she spends as much time with him as she can. Even our Saturdays are now cut to once a fortnight.
I was slowly beginning to consider going out with Frankie for the company, and the friendship. But my only problem would be that I'm sure Frankie has much more on his mind.
At home mum has begun to take more of an interest in my love life since Steve and I finished. Maybe she feels sorry for me.

" Ye need tae get oot mair? " Mum insisted.

" Och, ma I'm no in the mood, " I replied.

I told her about Frankie, and she seemed eager that I give him an opportunity to reveal his true character.

" But ah hev a feeling he's jist a charmer, " I said.

" Gee him a chance, before ye crucify him. "

" I'll think aboot it, " I said considering the prospect.

Sylvia sees Frankie every day at work, and he overwhelms her with compliments. It comes as no surprise to me that she thinks Frankie is fantastic; she's completely sold on his patter.

" Good morning, Sylvia yer looking gorgeous the day, " Frankie said holding the door open for Sylvia as she entered the King's.

" Ouch Frankie, ye say that every day, " Sylvia said laughing at his remarks.

" Aye ah know, but its true, " he said as he winked his eye.

Sylvia has been amazing through all my turmoil, she has listened to me endlessly every day at work going on, and on about how Steve has deceived me. She's wiped my tears, and helped me on the road to recovery. She's been a ROCK! And I am so grateful for her support.

" Patsy, Frankie's such a lovely boy, what harm would one date do? " Sylvia was trying her very best to encourage me to take that first initial step to move forward with my life. I know she means well, and only wants me to be happy.

" I'll think aboot it, " I said, and I did intend to give it a lot of thought.

Linda was also harping on, and on at me to go out with Frankie. I guess I have nothing to lose. I ought to try to make a new life without Steve. I need to get out of my room, and change the song on my record player to a HAPPY song....

CHAPTER 34

Frankie

I finally agreed to go out with Frankie. After all he did have all the patter. And he was good looking. He sashayed around the theatre as if he owned it. I knew he was a bit full of himself. But I needed a diversion from thinking about Steve.

I recognized that it wasn't healthy for me to stay in my room, and play heartrending songs on my record player every night for the rest of my life. And my big worry was that I would become so depressed; I may eventually end up in Bellsdyke (a mental institution just outside of Glasgow) I felt that BAD!!!

I knew I had to do something quick or they would be taking me away in a grey van, and throwing away the key.

Frankie and I met up on Saturday night, and he took me to my first Chinese Restaurant, and we both had a curry. I didn't really enjoy the food. It was far too hot and spicy for me. I was accustomed to plain old Scottish cuisine (mince an tatties), but Frankie didn't seem to mind the heat he devoured every drop.

" Dae ye no like it Patsy?" He asked.

" Well, naw, it's no really ma cup o' tea, " not wanting to complain, and seen to be ungrateful.

" Well dinnae eat it. "

" Ah dinnae like tae leave it, " I said feeling slightly uncomfortable.

" Its aw right, don't worry, aboot it, " Frankie said concerned that I might be a bit embarrassed.

We chatted away like old pals while we drank our Cona coffee, and mints. (The best part of the meal) Having a common interest in the King's gave us plenty of scope to blether on about all the famous celebrities.   Frankie worked in close contact with most of the stars, and he had the opportunity to get to know their likes, and dislikes so he knew all the scandal that was going on behind the scenes. After all, it was his job to make sure the artiste's had everything they needed.

" Ma favourite is Francie, and Josie, I love their act. And Francie always gees me a big tip, " Frankie boasted.

" Aye, ah think their great tae. "

Frankie was a bit of a comedian himself. He told me a lot of funny stories, and he did make me laugh, but although we were deep in conversation, and I was laughing at all

Frankie's jokes; Steve still never left my mind the whole night.

Going home on the bus, he put his arm around me. But it felt like a heavy load on my shoulders, and I instantly wanted to push it off, but I didn't want to embarrass Frankie or me. What a relief to get off the bus, and be free from his arm around my neck.

When we at last arrived at the entrance to my close I knew that he thought he was in for a winching session, (kissing in Scotland) but I wasn't ready to be kissed by Frankie, or anyone else. I just wanted to run up the stairs.

As we entered the tenement, Frankie looked a bit shocked when I said very quickly before he could get comfortable with his surroundings.

" Thanks for a great night, ah need tae go cause I'm bursting fir a pee, " I lied as I hastily made my way towards the stairs. Twisting my legs in all directions pretending to be desperate for the toilet.

" Whit! " The disappointment was written all over his face.

" Aye it must have been aw that coffee. It's a diuretic, ye know, " I said walking quickly.

" Whits a DIURETIC! Can ye no wait a wee minute? " Frankie asked as he was walking behind me frantically trying to catch up to my pace.

" Sorry, Frankie ah need tae go PAL! " I said as I was going up the stairs two at a time.

" Och aw right...Cheerio then, " He shouted sounding a bit disenchanted by my rushed departure.

" Aye, cheerio, " I roared back as I reached the top of the stairs, and glad to be free of his company.

When I opened the door all the lights were out indicating that mum, and dad must already be in their bed. GOOD! I went straight to my room pleased to be alone with my own thoughts.

I lay in bed reflecting on the time spent with Frankie. It wasn't a particular great night, but it wasn't the worst date I've been on. Frankie was entertaining, and did seem more genuine than I gave him credit, but he wasn't Steve. And I'm not sure if I would ever want to repeat it.

Maybe it was too soon, and I just need some more time. I fell asleep wondering what Steve was doing. I will need to give myself a good talking to. I can't possibly continue to grieve for someone who doesn't want me in his life.

WHEN! OH! WHEN! Will this hurt ever disappear from my heart???

CHAPTER 35

The Roses

Frankie continued to repeatedly pester me into going back out with him, but I felt that I still needed a bit more time before I ventured into another relationship. I was hurting and until I was able to let go of my pain there was no point in getting involved with anyone. It wouldn't be fair on them or me.

" Patsy, do ye fancy a wee night at the jigging on Saturday? " Frankie asked as I was leaving the King's to go home.

" No thanks, I'm babysitting fir ma brother, " I lied.

" I'll baby-sit we ye, if ye like? "

" Sorry, but ye might scare the poor wain's. "

" Aw Patsy, yer a hard wuman, a've got tickets for the Billy Connolly show next week if ye fancy going, " he asked, and waiting eagerly for my reply.

" Naw, ah don't think so, " I said using a firm tone to try to get it through to him that I wasn't interested, and he was wasting his time.

Frankie's disappointment was evident in his sad expression, I felt bad that I had rejected him yet again, but I couldn't help it. I just can't seem to be able to say YES!
I met up with Linda on Saturday. We were sitting in our usual booth, blethering away ten to the dozen.

" There's a new comedian doing a show at the King's the noo, and everyone is bragging aboot how great he is, " I said tucking into my fish supper.

" Whit's his name, ah might go and see him, we John. "

" Billy Connolly. "

" Och ah saw HIM! On the Michael Parkinson show the other night, he wis brilliant, " Linda explained all excited remembering how much Billy Connolly had made her laugh.

" Frankie's got tickets for his show next Saturday, and he wants me tae go we him. "

" Why dae ye no gee him another chance. It's been almost a year now since ye heard fae Steve. Ye need tae move on now Patsy yev only got ONE life. And ye will hev a great night oot watching Billy Connolly. "

" Aye, ah KNOW! Ah'll think aboot it. "

" PROMISE!!! Me ye will. Promise? " Linda said with a pleading look in her eyes.

" AYE! Aye, ah PROMISE! "

I arrived home to find a huge bouquet of beautiful red roses sitting on the kitchen table. My heart missed a beat. My first thoughts even after all this time; Has Steve sent them? How crazy am I?
Steve I imagined would have an incontestable explanation for abandoning our love, and a note with the roses would confirm the reason WHY! He never got in touch for so long.
I still can't believe, I'm still having nightmares, and clinging to a dream that perhaps... Steve had been hit by a car, and is in a coma stuck in some hospital ward somewhere suffering from amnesia, and unable to contact me, or he's got an incurable disease, and doesn't want me to know he's dying.
Obviously, I have watched far too many old black and white movies. Especially the film " An Affair To Remember " where Deborah Kerr gets hit by a car as she rushes frantically to meet Cary Grant the love of her life. He's left waiting at the top of the Empire State Building unaware of the accident. When she fails to meet him; he assumes that she has stopped loving him. She doesn't contact him because her legs were severely damaged by the car, and she doesn't want him to know that she will never be able to walk again. He finds her in the end, and

they both live happily ever after. Why am I still clinging onto HOPE!!

Here I am, a basket case, forever waiting and praying, that Steve will come back into my life, and everything will be perfect, and we will walk away into the sunset and live happily ever after...

I awoke from my minute of madness and quickly opened the tiny white envelope. My heart hoping that there could actually be a happy ending, and the love of my life still loved me. On the card were the words.

Patsy,
I bless the first day I saw you.
Please, please give me another chance. Come with me to see Billy Connolly on Saturday night. Please!!!

LOVE Frankie xxx

I burst in to tears, and let the card fall to the floor. What a fool I have BEEN! I have subconsciously been living in a fantasy world. I needed this wake up call to shock me back to reality.

I'm now determined that there will never, ever be any more tears shed for Steve. He's hurt me far too much, and for too long. It's now time to move on with my life, at LAST!

CHAPTER 36

1975

Carol and I were very close for almost two years, and at the beginning we couldn't get enough of each other. I really liked her, but to be honest it was definitely more a lust for each other. Love was never on our agenda. We just wanted to have as much fun as we could. And we did. But, I think we both knew there was something MISSING! In our relationship.

Then as time went on we saw less and less of each other, and we just seemed to slowly drift apart. Carol, had finished her art degree, and wanted to widen her prospects of becoming an art designer. And I'm certain, although we never discussed it, that London was always on the top of her list to further her career. I had an inkling that she would never remain in Halifax, so it wasn't a big shock when she informed me that she was moving to London.

Our relationship had reached an amicable end, but I was still sorry to see her go. I would miss her friendship, but I also admired her to be moving in the direction she believed in. Carol is reaching out for her dream, and I can't help but respect her self-belief. I'm sure she will become the next Vivienne Westwood one day. And I know we will always remain good friends.

Pete, the self confessed bachelor is now married to a wonderful girl called Susan, and he has a little baby girl, and another one on the way. After all his theories about LOVE! Being just a gimmick, and that he would never succumb to something so frivolous. Well all his convictions were squashed when he met his future wife, and she changed his outlook completely. He's a very lucky man to have found the love of his life.

ME! Well I have managed to fulfil part of my dream, and am now working as a junior doctor at Halifax General Hospital. But my main field of interest is in surgery, and I am now eager to spread my wings, and become a surgeon.

Lately I have been doing a lot of research into the best hospital to train as a surgeon. London's Royal Mars den Hospital is probably the best there is, but it is extremely difficult to be accepted.

The Glasgow Royal Infirmary also has an established reputation for excellence. And is also a very popular hospital, and not so easy to get into. Being accepted by either would be amazing. I am hedging my bets, and sending my CV to both hospitals, and I'm hoping at least one of them will consider me as a good candidate.

Mum has found love again, and is now in a long-term relationship with a very nice man called George. At first it was difficult for Anna, and I to accept that mum would even deem to consider another man after dad. But after a lot of deliberation, and heartache, Anna, and I both realised that we were being very selfish, and began to realize that mum is entitled to be happy, and to have someone special in her life.

George is a kind man, and he has created a miracle by making the sadness disappear from mum's eyes. Mum looks radiant, and very happy with her life. Something I thought could never be possible ever again.

Having George around also relieves me of my responsibilities as head of the family. I can continue my studies without worrying if mum and Anna are being looked after. And if I am lucky enough to be accepted for either London or Glasgow it will make leaving them a lot easier knowing they are safe.

Anna, I have to say, although it's difficult to imagine, has grown into a sensible teenager. She is hoping to receive first-rate results in her exams, and then hopefully head off to university in the near future. I'm sure she will do well. She is a bright kid, and very determent and ambitious.

I've been patiently waiting for over three months now for a response to my applications. I know that it is a slow process, but as it is coming closer to the starting dates for both hospitals. I'm becoming extremely impatient, and nervous; as each day approaches hoping soon that there would be a reply to my submission.

Lately, I have changed my tactics, and stopped running down to catch the post every day. I have realised over the years of waiting for letters that you can't rush these things. It doesn't help the situation; you just have to remain patient.

I walked into the hall as mum was picking up the letters from the mat. She quickly scanned through them, and handed me two envelopes. One brown, and one white, the brown one was from the tax, and the white one was far more interesting, I knew instantly it was from London by the postscript. This is IT!

I hesitated before I tore open the envelope. Mentally I said a short prayer in my head before I ripped it apart. PLEASE! PLEASE! Say YES! Hoping, and wishing; that I had been accepted for the job. I read the letter quickly, it was short, and sweet, explaining they had filled their quota for the year, but regretted that I did not fit the criteria for the post at this time, but I could try again next year. I was GUTTED!

I now had to pin all my hopes on Glasgow. If Glasgow refused me, then I guess I could apply again next year. I won't be put off. I'm determined that I'm going to be a surgeon one day.

I walked into the kitchen the letter still in my hand. Mum was filling the kettle with water at the sink.

" Well son, what does it say? " Mum asked.

" London are not interested in another Dr. Christian Barnard, " I said trying to hide my disappointment.

" Not to worry son, you still have Glasgow, perhaps they will be their looking for another Alexander Fleming? " She said smiling.

" But mum, he's not a SURGEON! He discovered penicillin, " I replied with a slight giggle.

" Oh, REALLY! I must be mixing him up with someone else, " we both burst out laughing.

Two long weeks later and a letter finally arrived, my prayers were answered. I was offered a job as a junior doctor in the gynaecology department at Glasgow Royal Infirmary. I was really excited about the prospects of furthering my career, and maybe becoming a great surgeon.

BUT! There was one draw back; I wasn't looking forward to leaving all my family and friends behind.

" Mum, I've been accepted for Glasgow Royal, " I shouted to mum, who was coming down the stairs.

" Oh, son I know it's what you want, and I'm pleased for you, BUT! I am going to miss you so much. "

Mum ran down the last few steps; to give me a big hug I could see tears dripping down her face from the corner of her eyes. I held her close for a moment, and then slowly I let her go.

" HEY! Glasgow's not that far, and I can drive it in about three hours, " I said encouragingly.

" I suppose so, " mum said as she wiped away her tears.

She stared into my eyes, and I could feel her scrutinizing my very soul, and a smile slowly emerged on her face telling me it was okay; I could go NOW! I wasn't a boy anymore.

Mum and Anna were understandably sad that I was leaving, but they were also thrilled that I had been accepted for my new post. They both realised the importance of this post, and how much I desperately wanted this chance to follow my destiny.

Mum had her new life with George, and Anna knew it was vital for her to have the same freedom, to be able to choose whatever she wanted to do in life. So she never made too much of a fuss, when I left.

Anna was aware that one-day she too would be following her own dream…

CHAPTER 37

Linda's Wedding Song

The roses did the trick, I finally succumbed to Frankie's constant attention, and I gave him the chance to express his true feeling. He, has exceeded my expectation, and has never disappointed me. Continually bombarding me with love and affection something I have always yearned for, and it's worked.

Our relationship has lasted for almost three years, and life's been really good. We've also managed to go on a couple of great holidays together at Butlin's Ayr with Linda and John who have now become our best friends.

Frankie's has been promoted to Theatre Manager, and I've also came up in the world to Wardrobe Assistant Manager. Not bad for a NOVIS! Granny Stewart, and I would have had a good laugh at my progress. But most important I'm certain she would have been proud of me.

Sylvia has now employed an extra member of staff, a young girl called Eleanor to help us with the increasing demand for elaborate costumes. She's only sixteen, but very keen to learn the trade, and it's great to have a spare pair of hands for the busy times.

Linda is getting married in a couple of weeks. She's a teacher now at our old primary school, and she adores working with the children. She was born to be a teacher she has such an easygoing nature. John's also a teacher, but in a secondary school, which can be very demanding, but he loves the challenge.

Recently Linda and I have been meeting up more often to discuss her wedding plans. But it's also been a great excuse to have a girly night in. Listening to music is still one of our favourite pastimes.

" Whit's left tae dae? " I asked as I ate my crisps sitting on top of Linda's bed.

" Och, it's aw done, me ma's been on the ball organizing the whole shebang, " Linda said very nonchalant as she filed her nails.

" Great, we can sit back, relax and hev another cider, " I said.

" There is one thing! Ye kin help me pick the music for the disco, " Linda said as she handed me a box of records.

" Aye, nae bother. "

Whilst I was raking through the records I began to feel a bit nostalgic remembering all the songs that Linda and I use to dance to, and all the good times we had. When suddenly I felt scared for Linda I had a horrible thought flash through my brain. What if my best pal was marrying the wrong guy?

" Linda are ye really SURE that yer not making a mistake? Are ye sure John's the ONE! " I blurted the words out recklessly; I already knew the answer. I just needed to be reassured I kind of lost the plot for a second.

" Don't be daft Patsy, I KNEW from the first time I saw John that he was the one, " Linda replied without any hesitation.

That's all I needed to hear. I was thrilled that Linda was happy, and about to embark on a new chapter in her life, and delighted that she still wanted me to be part of it.
We spent the rest of the night trying to agree on what song should be played for the first dance.

" Whit aboot " Long And Winding Road, " I said

" Naw, that's too depressing, and anyway John loves Elvis it his tae be an Elvis song, " she said appearing a bit exasperated at not instantly coming up with a song to suit.

" Well then, " Its Now Or Never. "

" Naw, that's no romantic enough, plus it sounds like I'm desperate, " Linda was getting more frustrated, and I'm sure the stress of the wedding was the cause.

" Whits his favourite Elvis song then? " I asked gently.

" The Wonder Of You " but a'm no sure if that would be aw right. Whit do ye think? "

" I think it's a perfect song and I'm sure John would be ecstatic with any song sung by Elvis, " I said with confidence.

" Yer right Patsy, whit would ah dae without ye, com'eer an give me a big hug."

Linda was now on a high, she jumped up and grabbed me hugging me tight against her as she bounced around the room, squashing my chest, and almost stopping my lungs from expanding.

I left Linda in a happy mood. And as I walked home slowly I reflected on the most important decision Linda will ever have to make in her life. I felt a great feeling of happiness, and contentment sweep over me for Linda's future. I now had no reservations as to whether John was good enough for my best buddy. Linda had convinced me that John is the best man for the job.

CHAPTER 38

Mums In Hospital

At home mum wasn't looking that well lately. She seemed to be always struggling to get her breath, and she hardly ate anything, but still appeared to be putting more weight on. I was beginning to sense that something wasn't quite right, and I was becoming really worried at the state of her health.

" Ma hev ye no been tae the doctor's yet? " I asked cautiously not wanting to upset her, as I knew she hated anyone thinking, she was weak.

" Nae need fir that I've jist got a wee cauld I'll be awright in a day or two, " mum wheezed out the words.

" Ye've been saying that fir weeks, " I emphasized.

" Aye, well it's ma body, " she croaked.

" I'll phone, and make an appointment fir ye if ye want? "

" Am no going tae the doctors so ye'll be wasting yer time, " mum said her eyes now filled with rage.

I couldn't force her to go to the doctors, but I could talk to Kirk, and ask his advice. Dad wouldn't be an option. If anyone could persuade mum to do something, it was Kirk. I phoned Kirk that night after mum had gone to bed, and he was a bit surprised when I explained mum's condition. But he told me not to worry he would deal with it.
Sure enough, the very next day Kirk swiftly took mum to the doctor's surgery.
Once the GP had finished with his examination he explained to mum that she needed some more tests, and he was going to arrange for any necessary scans, and an x-ray to be done immediately.
It was only about a week later, when I returned home after a final fitting of my slightly too tight bridesmaid dress, to find a short note lying on the kitchen table.

Gone tae the Royal Infirmary we yer ma.

Da.

I was supposed to be going to Linda's hen night. I immediately phoned her.

" Linda, am sorry ah don't know if am gon'nae make it the night, ma's been taken to the royal infirmary. "

" Don't worry yer sel Patsy, it can't be helped I hope yer ma gets better, " Linda said.

" I'll try and catch up we ye later, I hope, " I put the receiver down and ran out the door.

When I arrived at the Royal Infirmary's emergency department, I was informed at the reception desk, that they had transferred mum to a gynaecology ward. I quickly found the ward, but when I entered her room I wasn't prepared for the sight before me. It was a total shock; mum was already in a bed hooked up to drips, and with an oxygen mask fixed onto her white face. She looked dreadful.
Dad was sitting at the side of the bed, reading the Daily Record, eating a chocolate biscuit, and drinking a cup of tea. I was disgusted. I walked past him, and sat at the other side of the bed.

" Ma! How are ye? " I asked gently as I sat on the chair next to her bed.

Mum slowly managed to open her tired eyes and glance in my direction, but then her eyelids closed again obviously far too heavy to stay open; she didn't even have the strength to say anything. I turned, and faced dad.

" Dad, whit's happening? " I asked him interrupting his full attention to the Daily Record.

" She'll be alright, she's been seen by a very nice doctor. He says she might need an operation? " He said without lifting his eyes from the newspaper.

" Whit kind of operation? " I was now angry at his attitude.

" Ye know, wuman's problems, " he replied, again not taking his nose out of the paper.

" When are they gonnae operate? " I bombarded him with questions.

" Och, ah don't know, soon, ah think, she's tae get some tests first, " he said.

But, unable to take the time to look in my direction. His main interest was the sports page, and how his precious football team were measuring up.

" Did ye phone anyone? " I asked getting out of my seat, and walking towards the door. I had to get out of the room I wanted to punch him for being an ignoramus.

" Naw. "

" Well, I'll go and contact the boys, since your obviously far too busy, " I said sarcastically.

" Ye better mind yer cheek, " he was now glaring at me dropping the newspaper onto the bed.

I hurriedly left the room, and went to phone the family. I managed to contact all three of my brothers. Kirk, and Fred said they would meet me at the hospital as soon as they could. But, Dean would take much longer, as he was going to drive down from London, and he probably wouldn't be here until tomorrow.
I phoned Frankie, and just caught him before he left for John's stag night. Poor Frankie, he wasn't sure what to do;

he wanted to come to the hospital to be with me. But I insisted that he go out with the boys.

" Aw, Patsy ye need me tae be we ye, I'll come straight over. "

" Naw! A'm aw right dinnie worry, jist ye go oot an enjoy yer self, wance ma's settled I'll catch up we Linda, " I said trying to convince Frankie that mum was going to be all right.

Kirk, and Fred were up at the hospital within an hour. They were both visibly shocked at mum's rapid deterioration, and were desperate to know the prognosis. Dad wasn't that clear in his interpretation of the situation, which annoyed Kirk immensely.

" Da, wits happening we ma, " Kirk asked in a threatening demanding manner.

" Ah, think there gonnae need tae operate, but I'm no too sure. "

" Ye THINK! That's no good enough a'm going tae find someone who know what's really happening, " Kirks anger evident, but controlled.

Kirk immediately stormed out of the room in search of a member of staff.
He was gone only a few minutes. We were all sitting very quiet around mum's bed when he came back into the room. Kirk then explained that he had spoken to a nurse.

" The doctor that's looking after ma is busy at the moment, but as soon as he's free he will come, and speak tae us, " Kirk revealed.

Mum had a small single room, and the four of us were sitting close to the bed. Mum seemed to be aware that we were there, but unable to communicate. I was holding mum's hand when the doctor entered the room.
I turned my head, and instantly became even more shocked! I squeezed mum's hand really tight without realizing what I was doing. Mum immediately roused out of her stupor and opened her eyes.

" It's awright, dinnae worry aboot me, " she mumbled, and then instantaneously fell back to sleep the second I released her damaged hand.

I dare not take another look I didn't want it to be him, and I deliberately kept my eyes focused on mum, but I was conscious that the doctor appeared flustered as he introduced himself.

" I'm, I'm, Steven Aitkin, I'm looking after your mother's care, " he said shaking Kirk's hand.

" I'm pleased to meet you, " Kirk replied.

OH! NO! It's him it's my STEVE! Fred also shook the doctors hand, I never moved, I sat glued to my seat, traumatized by his presence, and deliberately trying to shut out his existence focusing on mum with all my mite. Where did he come FROM? I feel sick. Oh! God what do I do NOW?

" If you, and your family want to come into my office, I'll give you an update on your mother's progress, " the doctor explained.

Kirk and Fred left with the doctor. But before leaving the room Fred glanced at me to see if I was coming. It was very clear that I had decided not to follow; as I never made any move to get up. Poor Fred was unaware of the added stress I was under and just assumed that I didn't want to go. In actual fact even if I wanted to go I don't think my legs would be able to support my body at this moment in time.

They weren't gone that long, but it was evident by their faces when they entered the room that it wasn't good news. I had to forget about my own feelings, and concentrate on what was happening to my mum. But it took all my willpower not to run after Steve, and ask him, WHY? WHY? WHY!

I wanted to know. I just needed to know WHY? He never answered ANY of my letters. But now is not the time.

When Kirk came back into the room, he sat down next to mum, and held her hand. Mum didn't make any respond. Kirk was visibly shaken by what the doctor had revealed, and I'm sure there were tears in his eyes. Fred, appeared to be less emotional, and ready to take charge of the situation.

" What did the doctor say? " I asked struggling with the words.

" Lets go, and get a wee cup o' tea, " Fred said as he led me out of the room into the corridor.

Kirk stayed behind his head now bowed down over his, and mum's hands.

I somehow regained my strength, and left with Fred. We walked along the never-ending corridors without saying a word until we reached the canteen. It seemed like an eternity dragging my heavy legs one at a time. We sat in the hospital café, and Fred proceeded to dissect what the doctor had revealed.

" Patsy, it's not good, ma is dying, " he whispered. I couldn't speak. Fred continued to do the talking.

" Mum has ovarian cancer, and they don't think it is possible to operate... The tumour has spread to her liver. There is nothing they can do for her... but make her comfortable, and pain free... " Fred slowly explained holding both my hands.

I only heard the word MUM'S DYING! And my mind shut down it was all far too much for my brain it was now overloaded. I lost control. I couldn't function. I could feel the blood drain to my feet. And it felt like someone had tied a tourniquet around my ankles blocking the back flow of blood reaching any of my arteries. I felt nauseated. I let out a YELL! And collapsed into Fred's arms.

Unable to stop the horrible screaming in my ears; I could hear the SCREECH! In the distance, of what sounded like a wounded animal.

Why did someone not help that poor soul? Not realizing the animal was ME!!!

My heart was aching for the mother I never had, and for my lost LOVE...

CHAPTER 39

Glasgow Royal

Arriving in Glasgow late at night, and seeing the City for the first time I suddenly felt alone. It was raining, and Glasgow, looked cold, and damp. Not one of the greatest ways to see any city.

I was tired after my journey, and my thoughts were not rational. I started to wonder if maybe I had made a mistake, and that I should have found a hospital nearer home.

I stopped the car, and shouted at a man in the street for directions, but unlike Glasgow's reputation for being tough the man was very friendly.

" Excuse me, do you know the way to the Glasgow Royal Infirmary, " I called.

" Aye son its no far fae here, straight up the road then turn left. Ye cannae miss it. It's big ENOUGH! "   He laughed.

He was right. It is a huge building of character dominating a large part of the street. Inside the hospital there was a maze of massive hallways, and stairs all going in different directions. My first impression was that it wasn't going to be an easy task finding my way around these many corridors.

Over the next few weeks I quickly adjusted to my new surroundings, and made friends with some of the other doctors. My residence's quarters were basic, but adequate. A room with my own shower, toilet, and a communal TV room with a small kitchen.

My post was extremely challenging, and I was gaining a huge amount of relevant experience. And, I was now positive I had made the right decision training to become a surgeon.

Glasgow had a lot of hidden music talent, and I was pleasantly delighted to find that the entertainment side of the city was second to none. I really appreciated live music, and nearly every pub in the town had a live band, with extremely gifted performers. Slowly I was adapting to the different culture, and loving every minute.

I would be lying if I said I never gave Patsy a thought, but I think it was only natural being in the same town. I was curious to know what she was up to, and secretly hoping that one-day I would bump into her. My anger for her had now gone. I felt it was a waste of an emotion to keep a grudge, best to let it go.

I was only in the post about a month, and still finding my feet on a busy ward. When I was asked to go, and speak to the family of one of my patients. Explaining to love ones that a member of their family was now terminally ill, and there is nothing medically that we can do now to stop the process. It's not an easy task, and one that every doctor dreads.

I walked into the room, and saw the family sitting around the bedside. The father whom I had spoken to earlier, and a man in his fifties I assume his son sitting beside him, and another man, and a girl sitting at the other side of the bed. The girl was holding her mother's hand. She looked across at me then quickly drew her attention back to her mother, who became conscious for a brief moment.

I only had a slight glance at the girl, I couldn't be sure if it was HER! Or not. But, I couldn't trust my reactions to take another look. I thought my worst nightmare was standing only five feet away from me. I couldn't let my brain react I had to turn away immediately. I focused on the father, and son.

My heart was jumping inside my body, my emotions were running riot I wanted to look her straight in the eye, and ask her WHY? She had lied.

HEY! What am I thinking? I'm a doctor. This is not about ME! Or PATSY!

My patient is dying; Mrs. STEWART is my priority I had to focus, and remember SHE! Is paramount in my mind, and is the one who needs my full attention. PATSY; could wait for another time.

I had to control the aggressive adrenaline rushing through my veins I could be over reacting. Maybe it's not PATSY! But why am I so EMOITIONAL? I thought all these feeling were gone, and buried in the past?

Emergency situations are something I am usually able to deal with instantly. But this is completely different from a life, and death situation. This is about someone you loved ignoring my feeling, KNOWING! How much I cared, but quite blatantly refusing to acknowledge my pleading, and left me to suffer. I can't believe after all this time that I can still feel the pain of losing Patsy. OH! GOD! And I thought I was OVER HER!

My professional training took over, and allowed me to conduct myself in the correct manner. But I was extremely relieved that the girl stayed in the room with her father, and only the two men followed me to my office.

Away from Patsy's presence I was able to compose myself, and explain to the brothers that their mother was seriously ill, and her prognosis was very poor. The brothers sat at my desk for a few minutes clearly distraught at the news.

" There must be something ye can dae? " Kirk pleaded.

" I'm sorry, but there's nothing we can do; we can only make her comfortable, and pain free, " I said softly.

" Are ye a hundred percent sure? " Tears now spilling from Kirks eyes.

" Nobody can be a hundred percent, but I know it doesn't look good, but I have to make you aware of the seriousness of the situation. We will do all we can for your mother, " I said tenderly.

" Thanks doc, " Fred said very composed. He got up from his chair, and helped his big brother out of the door.

Once alone in my office, I sat there feeling I had just been hit by an express train. I'm not stupid, I knew being in the same city as Patsy; there would always be a slight possibility that I would perhaps one day bump into her, at club or in the town.

But I wasn't expecting it to be at the hospital where I worked. And even worse I never imagined for a second that I would be the doctor looking after Patsy's dying mother. If only I had been accepted for London's Royal Mars den then this would never have happened.

I was totally unprepared for the situation; I never realised that I would react in such a frantic way. I had convinced myself that she wouldn't have ANY! Effect on ME!

GOOD GOD! Who was I KIDDING?

CHAPTER 40

I Still Can't Believe Mum's So Ill

Fred managed to calm me down, and guide out of the hospital, and into his car, but my head was in turmoil. Sitting in the back seat, I know I should have been concentrating on mum's illness, and how we were all going to cope with her dreadful diagnosis.

But I couldn't help myself, all I could think about was Steve. And, Why? Oh! WHY? Of all the hospitals in the world did Steve have to choose to work in Glasgow; He's the last thing I need in my life right now.

My mum is lying in a hospital bed, and may only have weeks to live. I have enough to contend with. I don't need STEVE adding to my problems. And anyway, I'm happy, and have a new love. It's taken me a l o n g; l o n g time to forget Steve, but I did it. And I have grown to love Frankie with all my heart, and we've even joked about getting married in the future.

I know at first, I had huge doubts about Frankie's infidelity; I thought he could never be faithful with his Italian good looks, and his gift of the gab, what women could refuse him. But he's proved me completely wrong. It has taken me what seems like an eternity to believe in him, but at last, I have finally realised, that I completely misjudged Frankie, and have discovered over the years what special qualities he possesses.

In all the time I have known him; he's never even looked at another woman. But what attracted me the most to Frankie has been his total obsession on his quest to win my heart. He never once gave up on me, and that's why I love so much.

If! I am happy, and content with my new life. Why? Am I so Upset? Why do I CARE; where Steve works? Or what Steve does in his life? Why, Oh why is he having such a disturbing effect on ME???

It wasn't easy putting Steve out of mind. Seeing him had opened up all my old wounds that I thought were healed. Oh God, I never realised for a second I could still have such uncontrollable anger towards him, even after all this time. I can't forgive him for the brutal finish to our relationship. And I wish, I could stop the desperate need I feel to ask him, face to face, WHY? Oh? WHY? Had he never bothered to answer any of my letters?

When I got home I went for a bath, and as I lay in the hot water I kept thinking this is madness. I need to give myself a shake, and forget Steve exists, and concentrate on my life at present with Frankie, and remember that Steve had his chance, but he didn't want me.

On Sunday, I called Linda to find out how her hen night went, and to apologize for missing her big night.

" Linda, ah'm sorry ah really wanted tae be there. "

" Och Patsy, Ah know that, but it could nae be helped I understand that ye hid tae be we yer ma. We can hev another night jist you and me, " Linda explained. I could tell by her shaky voice that she was trying to be brave for me, and she was holding back the tears.

" How did it go, were ye drunk? " Changing the subject, and trying to lighten the mood.

" It wis fantastic we went on a pub crawl, and I collected aboot a hundred pounds, but ye shood hev seen the punters, some o' them looked like they were on there last legs coughing, and spurting their beer all over the place, so ah made them kiss me on the cheek. Ah wis nae taking any chances, " Linda said obviously enjoying the whole build-up of excitement to her wedding.

" A'm glad ye had a great night, I'll catch up we ye during the week. I better phone Frankie, and see if he's recovered fae the stag. "

" Nae bother Patsy, give your ma my love, bye the noo, "

I put the receiver down, and proceeded to call Frankie. The phone rang out for ages, and then finally I could hear a voice in the distance.

" Hello, " Frankie managed to say.

" Hi there it's me Patsy, ye sound rough. "

" A'm no well, the stag night was a riot, everyone wis challenging each other on how many whiskies they could drink. Ah don't know whit ah wis thinking, ah wis caught up in the spirit o' things and wis downing far too many half's. The best o' it is, ah don't even drink whiskey. "

" Listen don't ye worry aboot it, a'm going up tae the hospital tae see how ma is. You go back tae yer bed, and I'll see ye later. "

" Are ye sure? Ah feel lousy not coming we ye, " Frankie protested.

" Dinnae be daft. If you come we me they might no let ye oot, " I actually found myself laughing at the state Frankie had got himself into.

Just as I put down the phone the front door bell rang. It was Fred; he had come to take dad and me up to hospital. Dad was still in bed recovering after a heavy night on the bevy. I told Fred sarcastically not to interrupt dad's beauty sleep, and to leave him behind to stew in his own self inflicted mess. I was still annoyed at dad for being so ignorant whilst mum was ill, lying in her hospital bed.

Fred and I sat with mum for about two hours, but there was no response. She never moved the whole time we were there, her eyes remained closed, but she did look peaceful, and was obviously pain free.

Dean arrived with Kirk, Helen, and the boys. We all hugged each other in the corridor outside mum's room, and some tears were openly shed. We spent the rest of the day taking turns to sit with mum. Dad didn't even have the decency to come up to the hospital.

He will, I'm positive, be enjoying the free invitation to go and get drunk, without any interference from mum. I honestly don't think he realizes the extent of mum's illness.

Steve, however didn't appear to be around. Thank GOD! At least I wouldn't have to come in contact with him today.

CHAPTER 41

The Confession

Why? Did I have the strangest feeling Patsy was angry with ME! Or maybe, she was just finding it difficult to cope, with the embarrassment of having to endure my presence, and perhaps didn't enjoy the prospect of maybe bumping into me in the corridor.

It almost felt like I was the one who had dumped HER! And not the other way around, I might be reading it all wrong, and the hostility I feel is not focused on me at all. And that the anger Patsy demonstrates when I enter her mother's room may not be anything to do with me, but simply could be due to the circumstances she is dealing with at present.

It must be one of the hardest things in the world to watch your mother die. I was now over the initial shock of seeing Patsy, and I wanted to show some compassion, and explain to her that I was genuinely sorry that her mum was so ill. I hungered to give Patsy a big hug, and clarify to her that it was okay. I wished her well. I wanted to say to her we were young; we all make mistakes. I forgive you lets be friends. But her coldness towards me has stopped me dead in my tracks. I can't interfere; Patsy has enough heartache in her life without me adding to her grief.

At least I know for certain that she did ignore my letters, and that she wasn't in a nasty accident, leaving her brain damaged which was one of my biggest fears.

I was sitting in my office drinking a well-earned cup of coffee, after finishing a busy ward round, when I heard a knocked on my door.

" Come in, " I shouted.

" Sorry to bother you doctor, but could you come, and have a wee word with Mrs. Stewart, she's been asking for you all week, but this is the first time you have been on duty, " the nurse emphasized.

" Oh! Em...Is there any chance she will accept another doctor? " I said reluctant to visit her in case Patsy was at her bedside.

" No, she's been specifically asking for YOU every time she's been conscious, I can't ignore her pleas any longer, " she said her words were full of compassion.

I went to Patsy's mum's room, and the nurse followed. Mrs. Stewart looked very sad, and I could see tears in her eyes. What a relief Patsy wasn't in the room.

" Are you sore, Mrs. Stewart " I asked as I entered the room.

" No, am wanting a wee word we ye on yer own son, " she said with a demanding tone.

Not a usual request from a patient, but because of the circumstances I couldn't refuse. She seemed very alert, and determined to have her own way.

" It's all right you don't need to stay, " I said to the nurse standing at my side. When she had left the room I sat down on the seat beside the bed.

" What is it Mrs. Stewart, what's wrong? " I asked softly.

" You're the fella that ma Patsy wis writing tae aw they years ago aren't ye? "

" Yes, yes I am " I said a bit bewildered at the question, and surprised that she had remembered my name after all this time.

" Aye, ah never forgot yer name. Steven Aitkin, and that day when they brought me in tae hospital, ah knew the minute ye said yer name that ye were the lad that wis gonnae be a doctor. The wan ma Pasty wis writing tae aw they years ago, " tears now slowly running down her cheeks.

" That was in the past. "

" Aye it wis, but it's aw ma fault that ye broke up, " tears now streaming down her face, as she began to sob.

" It's not anyone's fault Mrs. Stewart, these things happen, don't upset yourself, " I said reassuringly.

" Son, ah hev tae confess before ah dee " she wheezed.

" Don't worry, it's okay, don't upset yourself, " I said, watching her as she struggled to catch her breath.

She went silent, and made a long sigh for what seemed like an eternity, and then with a determined effort she continued. The atmosphere was tense, and I was wondering what she could possibly want to say to ME!

" Promise me no matter whit a tell ye, that ye'll tell Patsy the truth, efter ah'm gone, promise ME? " Gripping my arms, and pulling me closer to her ear obviously very distressed, and determined that I hear every word.

" Yes, YES! OK! " I said hesitant wondering what she could possibly have to confess to ME! Her finger nails now digging deep into the flesh of my arm causing it to bleed.

" Promise me; PROMISE ME!! "

She was now losing complete self-control of her emotions; she began to weep, and howl unable to sustain her feelings. She must have used all her strength to sit up, and was now frantically trying to get herself out of the bed.

" All right, all right, but you need to calm down, and rest," I said easing her back on to the pillows.

" Ah'm, awfay sorry, but! BUT! BUT! Ah kept aw yer letters…And ah kept aw Patsy's letters tae. Ah wis suppose tae post them, BUT…. well Ah didnae! " She blurted out quickly between taking in gulps of air to allow her to continue to talk, and rid herself of this huge burden.

Next minute she was fighting with me to get out of the bed, I was holding her in my arms supporting her body, stopping her from falling to the floor, and at the same time trying to make some sense of her confession.
This statement came totally out of the blue, and was completely unexpected. I was incapable of digesting the full impact of what she had revealed. I was absolutely dumbstruck. But I was swiftly shocked back into reality when the door opened, and in walked Patsy. She was obviously confused and shocked at the scene that greeted her. I was still holding her mum, and she was rocking, and wailing in my arms.

" WHIT'S! Wrong! Are ye alright ma? " She asked very concerned, and deliberately avoiding looking in my direction.

Mrs. Stewart realising that Patsy was in the room very quickly leaned back onto her pillows, and then turned to face Patsy.
It was amazing to observe she had stopped crying almost instantly, and was now smiling at her daughter. What a performance.

" Ah wis feeling a wee bit sorry fir ma sel that's aw, and this kind doctor wis jist trying tae help me " she sniffed.

" Ah ma I'm sorry I wisnae here when ye needed me, but ah missed the bus, " Patsy explained, and totally ignoring my presence.

You could cut the atmosphere with a knife. I felt that I was invisible; I had to get out of the room. But at the same time I wanted to STAY, and say how sorry I was for not trusting her; Sorry for not trying harder; Sorry for believing that Patsy could lie to me. But this wasn't the time or place. Patsy's mum was dying, and I needed to respect that, I started to walk towards the door.

" Thanks doctor! " Mrs. Stewart said almost in a whisper, but visibly exhausted after her emotional confession.

" Its okay ma I'm here now, the doctor needs to get on with his work. He must be VERY BUSY!! " Patsy emphasized without even a glance towards the door in which I was leaving.

But now I know the reason why she is angry. And Patsy has every right not to want anything to do with me she believes I was the love rat who stopped writing. Leaving her without an explanation for ending our very special relationship.
I reluctantly walked out of the room, my heartbeat was racing, and the veins in my neck were bulging under the high pressure of the sudden increased blood flow to my heart; I wanted Mrs. Stewart to tell Patsy the truth NOW! And I wanted to hold Patsy, forever. But it was an unrealistic demand.
A woman was at the end of her life, and that woman is Patsy's mum, and any interference from me would not be appropriate. But why did this lady play God with our lives? What was her motive? What kind of a woman would do such a horrible thing to her own daughter?

Once in my office I sat staring into space, traumatized by the information I had just received. Unsure of what the outcome would be. If only I could go back in time, and take that train journey to Glasgow. The one everyone talked me out of going on. Why did I listen to them I should have had more faith in Patsy. I would have found out the truth, and who knows we could still be together.

Most of my life I have been able to work out what to do for the best. When dad died I took on the role as head of the family, looking after mum and Anna. Our cat died, and I buried it in the bottom of the garden. I wanted to become a surgeon; I search to find the best available hospital.

I knew it would be tough being separated from my family, and friends, but I also recognized that it would be a good opportunity for me. It was, I thought at the time the right thing to do.

But now, I'm not so sure. I'm faced with the biggest dilemma of my life; and I feel completely alone. I wish my family, and friends were here to help, and support me with my decision.

What should I do? Do I tell the only girl I have ever loved that her dying mother betrayed our love? Exposing her mother's evil deed?

Or do I say NOTHING???

And not cause Patsy any more anguish. And break my PROMISE...

CHAPTER 42

LINDA'S WEDDING

Mum was now gravely ill, and she was drifting in and out of consciousness. I was rushing about like a mad woman; running from work straight to the hospital, and then back home. Trying to be at work and at mum's bedside most of the day, wasn't an easy task. And I know the rest of the family was also struggling with the situation.

I'm glad Dean took some time off work, and remained in Glasgow; he didn't want to stay with dad, and me, preferring to reside at Kirk's house instead. Dean was able to spend time sitting with mum during the day while we were all at work. Then Dean would get a break knowing we were taking turns with the nighttime visit.

Dad was being really difficult, and spending more, and more time at the pub rather than visit mum in hospital. My bothers were not amused with his behaviour, but all three of them were avoiding a scene not wanting to upset mum.

But although all my free time was spent at my mum's bedside, I still managed to fulfil my role as a bridesmaid at Linda's wedding. And, Oh! God! I must have lost weight with all the stress, because the dress was now far too big, and there was no time to have it altered. I'm really glad it had these huge puff sleeves (which I hated) but could now hide my skinny arms.

On the big day, I went around to Linda's house to put on my bridesmaid dress. And although I had been with Linda and her mum when Linda chose her wedding dress; I knew it was gorgeous, but when Linda appeared from her bedroom standing in the hall with her full wedding regalia; her veil, diamond tiara, and her gorgeous black hair pinned up in an elegant Grace Kelly hairstyle, and her eyes had a special sparkle, which can only come when you are ecstatically happy, and contented.

OH! GOD! What a sight, I was stunned, and cried tears of happiness along with her mum and dad. Her beauty overwhelmed us all. Linda is a truly beautiful bride; she is stunning and looked just like a princess in her beautiful white gown.

I was standing in the church watching Linda take her vows. Frankie was at my side gently holding my hand. He has been my rock, my knight in shinning armour, and yet my thoughts have not been entirely focused on Frankie.

Since I saw Steve in the hospital, I have been totally distracted. I know, deep down in my soul that it's insane what I'm feeling, but I somehow can't help myself, and am unable to resist the temptation of thinking about the past.

My brain keeps showing me images of Steve and I standing outside my chalet watching the sunrise, or sitting on our special bench at the beach clinging to each other, never wanting to let go. I can't help remembering how I felt all those years ago. I'm still staring at Linda, but I'm seeing nothing. I've been transported into another world.

" Patsy! Patsy! Are ye awright? " I could hear Frankie say as he squeezed my hand.

" Aye, Aye, " I answered awakening from my trance.

As soon as I realised I had allowed myself to think about Steve in the middle of Linda's wedding. I felt the guilt overwhelm me. I could feel my heart bulge with grief, but it wasn't for my mum.

" Ah no it's no easy, but try an no think aboot yer ma the noo, " Frankie whispered in my ear, and kissing me lightly on the cheek.

I held his gaze and smiled. If he only knew where my thoughts were. I felt so ashamed Frankie was so good to me. He deserved better.
It was a glorious day; the sun never left the sky for one second, unusual for Scottish weather. And, as I glanced across at Linda now sitting beside her new husband, both of their faces beaming with happiness, I knew Linda had made the perfect choice.

" Linda, congratulations ye look beautiful pal, " I said giving her a big cuddle.

" Thanks Patsy, I'm glad ye could make it, " hugging me back.

" I would nae miss it fir the world. "

We were sitting at the top table totally full to bursting after eating a big plateful of steak pie, and potatoes. All the speeches were funny, and complimentary to the happy couple, but it was Linda's dad who had all the guests reaching for their hankies.

He proceeded to tell the story of his feelings of happiness when Linda was born, and how he adored her, and has watch her grow into a wonderful human being. He emphasized how proud he was of his precious little princess, and that he felt honoured to be her dad. I could see a tear appear on Linda's face, but she managed to contain herself, and glanced over at her dad with a loving smile on her face.

Quickly the best man, afraid that the atmosphere was becoming too emotional, stepped up, and proposed a toast to the new Mr. And Mrs. Peel. Everyone gave a big CHEER! And I'm certain they were all pleased for the swift change of mood.

All the guests were now caught up in the happy moment, and the magic continued as the DJ started to play Linda, and John's wedding song.

Elvis Presley's " The wonder of you. "

Linda and John left their seats, and walked slowly on to the dance floor, and all the guests gave them a round of applause. We gave them a few minutes to themselves before the best man, and I joined them on the dance floor.

Frankie, and I left the reception early to call on mum; we didn't want to miss a visit. Time was now so very precious, and we wanted to spend as many hours as we could with mum.

I never mention to Linda that I had seen Steve. I couldn't risk upsetting her, and spoiling her big day. It just wouldn't be fair, Linda's going on honeymoon tomorrow, and she doesn't need to know about any of my troubles. I am a big girl now, and should be able to deal with it myself.

Mum is deteriorating rapidly, and she is unconsciousness most of the time. The family has now decided that we should all take turns to visit mum so she's never left alone.

At work Sylvia has very kindly suggested that I could have some special leave of absence from work, giving me more time to be at mum's bedside.

" Patsy, ye need to take some days off to be with your mum. Ye look worn out, " she said firmly.

" Och, are ye sure Sylvia? Whit about the new costumes for the Stanley Baxter Show? " I asked a bit concerned about the workload.

" Eleanor, and I will manage, don't you worry. Now away home we ye, and try to rest before you collapse, " Sylvia said hugging me tight.

" Thanks Sylvia yer a great help, " I whispered into her ear as I hugged her back.

" Let me know how you get on, " Sylvia shouted as I was going out the door.

On the way out I caught up with Frankie who was about to start his afternoon shift. I explained to him that Sylvia has given me time off to be with mum.

" That's great Patsy, yer in need o' a break. I'll see ye later honey, " he gave me a huge cuddle, and a wee kiss.

CHAPTER 43

Mum's Torment

Over the last few days, during every visit that I was alone with mum, she appeared to be agitated, and disturbed about something. She kept tossing, and turning in her bed obviously having a bad dream, possibly about some event that happened in her life. She kept repeating the same words over and over again. It was heartbreaking to watch her struggle with her thoughts.

" Ah'm sorry, ah didnae mean it, I'm sorry! Ah'm sorry! Hen, " she kept crying out to me.

" It's okay ma I know, I know. "

" I shood never huv done it. It wisnae fair, forgive me, forgive me Patsy, " mum ranted.

" It's okay, its okay, hush now, go back to sleep, and have a wee rest, " I said as I massaged the fingers of her hand.

She would slowly settled down and drifted back to sleep.
Then on one particular visit, she became very restless, screaming, and shouting out, but it was impossible to make sense of the howling. At one point she almost fell out of the bed. The nurses heard all the commotion, and ran into the room. They attended to her immediately, and gave her an injection to help calm her down.
Mum, after about ten minutes appeared to be more at peace. I held her hand as she slipped into a sound sleep.
But, it was so tragic to witness mum lose her battle against this disease. She's been perpetually in total command of all her faculties throughout her whole life, but now the battle is too great, she's lost the fight. I only hope for her sake that her suffering is not prolonged.
I was sitting at her bedside, stroking her hair as she slept, when she suddenly opened her eyes. Staring directly at me, tears swelled out from her tired weary eyes, and then slowly rolled down her pale cheeks. She sat straight up in bed, and for a fleeting moment she looked alert, and in control of her senses.

" Patsy, I'm sorry, I wis wrang, I shoodnae done it. It wis a bad thing that ah did, " she said, but she wasn't ranting this time. She was calm, almost too calm.

" It's, alright ma, I forgive you, " I said softly.

" Do, ye really? Do ye! "

" Aye, of course ah dae, don't upset yer sel anymair. "

" But ye don't understand? " She was now grabbing my wrists.

" Ah do, its okay ma, let it go, it disnae matter anymair, " I said pleading with her to settle down.

" But hen, are ye happy? "

" Aye ma. "

" Are ye sure? "

" Aye, ma, I'm certain, now don't upset yerself anymair, please, " I said insistently, but gentle at the same time trying to make her understand that it was all right.

" Och, Thanks Hen, " she smiled, and all the tension seemed to leave her body; she immediately relaxed, and fell back into a deep sleep.

As I watched her close her tired worn out eyes, I gently wiped her tears away. She began to relax, and now looked at peace with her thoughts. I was pleased that I had managed to stop her torment, and was able to make her feel better.
A chill suddenly ran down my spine, I knew instantaneously at that moment she had taken her last breath, and DIED...

CHAPTER 44

The Little Black Box

It was about two weeks after the funeral, when I finally decided to sort out mum's clothes, and all her other bits and pieces. As nobody else in the family was willing to take on the job, I felt that it was something best done now rather than later. I packed all her clothes into boxes for the charity shop.

Being the only girl I was given all mum's jewellery; she didn't have anything of great value except her wedding, and engagement ring, which was all I kept for sentimental reasons. I would give the rest of her jewellery to Aunty Joan.

Mum, had an old battered brown cardboard type suitcase where she kept, photos, postcards, and some momentoes. I remember when I was a wee girl having a nosey at all the old photos. I got caught once, and got a clout on the ear from mum for rummaging through her precious souvenirs.

I remember one time Linda and I sneaked a wee look when mum was out, we fell on to the floor in fits of laughter as we looked at some of the old-fashioned clothes, and hairstyles, and also the regimented way everyone sat bolt upright when having their photo taken. They all seemed so scared of the camera, causing him or her to forget to smile. Sadly even granny Stewart's famous smile was never captured on camera. What a shame!

I sat on the bed, and studied the case contemplating whether I should have a look; I was a bit apprehensive at first to take a peek inside, although the fear of being caught was now, not an option anymore.

But it still felt really weird having the power to inspect mum's keepsakes; it felt a little eerie opening the case alone in her room sitting on her bed. But I wanted to feel her near to me; I know we were never close, not the way a mother, and daughter should be. But she was still my mum, and in a strange way I did miss her.

I opened the case, and slowly began to examine the photos of all the members of my family. Scrutinizing the ones of me as a baby. My favourite one was of me sitting on mum's knee; all togged up in a pink frilly dress, I must have been about one year old. I gave the impression that I was a little angel, and mum had such a proud expression on her face as she held me. I never saw any of that pride when I was growing up. I wonder WHY?

I sat, and read some of the old postcards sent when the families were on their holidays. One from granny Stewart when she was at Blackpool, and oh, there's one from me at Filey.

Dear Mum, and Dad

I'm having a great time here in sunny Scarborough with Linda. Wish you were here.
See you when I get back.

Patsy xx

God! I remember writing that postcard lying on the beach at Scarborough Linda and I had a great laugh at the obvious lie. It seems such a long time ago, and so unreal. I was about to close the case when I noticed a little black box. I tried to open it, but it was locked. That's ODD!! Then I recalled that I had seen a tiny silver key amongst the jewellery I was going to give to Aunty Joan.

Why did she have a box with a key? I WONDER? I was becoming extremely curious I quickly searched for the key amongst the jewellery. I found it hidden under mum's treasured pearls, the ones I hated. I was delighted to find that the key fitted the lock. Oh! What could be inside the box?

I became quite excited at the prospect of encountering a family secret, or a valuable piece of jewellery. I carefully opened the box, and the first thing I saw was a little red pouch, tied with ribbon and as it fell onto my lap I picked it up, and I quickly opened it, hoping for some diamonds, but what a disappointment it was dads STUDS!

At least a dozen for dad's shirt collars. I sniggered to myself remembering the huge protests dad made to mum about never being able to find his precious studs. She always denied any knowledge of their whereabouts. The cheeky little devil! She had hid them just to annoy him. Good for HER!

But! When I looked closer at the rest of the contents of the box. My cheerfulness stopped immediately, and my mood changed instantly. I screamed in HORROR! As I stared astonished at what I saw inside the box.

oooooOH!! G O D!! For a minute I forgot to BREATHE!!

My brain stopped functioning I couldn't comprehend what was in front of my eyes. I closed the lid; I quickly inhaled in gulps of oxygen to kick-start my brain. I gripped the lid of the box, slowly opening it again. Hoping I had made a mistake. My hands were shaking, and my heart was pounding I felt the pressure build up inside my body. I was now insanely angry. WHY? WHY? WHY?
My head was SCREAMING! I threw the box across the floor. And all the contents scattered out over the carpet.

My LETTERS!!! To Steve, and oh my GOD!!! OH! GOD! Steve's letters to me none of them opened. Why had she NOT posted them, and why had she kept Steve's letters from ME! How could she be so cruel?

OH! No!! Mums last words came back to me in a flash SORRY! That was why she repeatedly said she was SORRY!! And I thought she was feeling guilty for not being a good MUM!
I wanted desperately to vex this ferocious anger at her that was exploding from inside of my body, but that was now impossible. I needed HER! Desperately! To explain to me WHY? OH! WHY had she done this terrible thing to ME!!
WHO GAVE HER THAT RIGHT!

I sat on the bed unable to move frantically trying to absorb my findings, and make some sense of the hidden letters, but it was impossible.

What am I going to do NOW? I can't believe that mum could keep our letters, and sit back, and wilfully watch my torment, knowing she was the one causing me all the pain. What kind of mother could so callously torture her own daughter? I never imagined she could be so malicious.

Good GOD! And I thought that dad was the EVIL one.

How could I be so stupid! How could I be so wrong! I trusted HER to post my letters. I should have known better. I should have taken the time to post them myself.

I lay down on mum's bed weeping on her pillow. My pain, so I intense that I felt I wanted to die, to put an end to the excruciating pain in my heart. But the tears were not enough to ease my suffering I was in a bad way, and I wasn't sure how I was going to handle this awful mess.

I don't know how long I lay there totally shocked, and bewildered at my findings, staring at the letters on the floor. But eventually I got off the bed, and picked up the letters one by one, and was holding them tight in my hands. Still uncertain what to do next? Unable to understand what her motive could have been.

Oh how I wish I could confront her, and ask her WHY! She did IT! WHY? WHAT did she expect to achieve?

Eventually the ache in my heart was beginning to ease, and I was becoming a little bit calmer. Slowly I began to reflect on mum's last few hours spent in the hospital. And! Despite the magnitude of her crime, in her defence, she did say she was SORRY! And she did continuously try to explain to me her misdeed, but I chose to ignore her pleas, and stopped her confessing; I told her to forget it.

What a FOOL! If only I had known, but I never thought for a second that she could be capable of conspiring into my life, and acting so selfishly.

But looking back to those last weeks of her life, her regret was visible. Her conscience must have been giving her nightmares, and she did appear to be truly repentant for what she had done.

Oh, NO! That's why Steve always looked so angry towards me; he thought I lied to him, and that I had just stopped writing, without giving him an explanation. What heartache had I caused him?

Oh! GOD! POOR Steve he must think I'm a cruel bitch for treating him so badly. If only he knew the real truth. My mother for whatever reason decided to take control of our relationship, and deliberately break up our romance.

I am at a loss, and I'm finding it extremely difficult to comprehend why she would interfere so brutally with my life. I doubt that I will ever be able to understand her reason for her meddling with my life. But my dilemma, now is where do I go from here?

I was still holding the letters in my hands I slowly put them back into the box. I walked out of the bedroom and closed the door taking the box with me. I could now only feel a great sadness, feeling that she had deliberately cheated me out of what could have possibly been the love of my life.

What do I do now? I have to take a long look inside my heart, and try to sort out my true feelings for Steve, and Frankie.

What a disaster this knowledge has turned my whole world upside down.

CHAPTER 45

The Unopened Letters

I can't believe it's been almost three weeks now, since mum died, and I still haven't told anyone about the letters. It's eating away at me I'm going out of mind trying to come to terms with the reality of the situation. I feel I have been transported into another world, and nothing is real anymore. The shock discovery has been incomprehensible.

I don't know what to do? My thoughts are all mixed up.

I was tempted to ask Sylvia's advice, but then had second thoughts, because I know how much she adores Frankie. And I'm certain her opinion would be totally biased towards Frankie, and I'm sure she wouldn't even consider Steve as a contender.

I also considered confiding in Fred, but he is also very fond of Frankie, and treats him like a brother. Fred I'm sure would be in Frankie's corner. I feel totally trapped, and boxed in.

I have to tell someone. I am desperate for advice on what to do next. I can't keep this to myself for much longer. I'm sure my head will explode if I try to conceal this secret for another second.

Linda's been back from her honeymoon for over a week, and I have purposely been avoiding her, not wanting to burden her with my problems. Knowing Linda, she would suss out straight away that I was holding something back, and I'm sure she would detect that there was something amiss and she would eventually squeeze it out of me bit by bit.

I was, however hoping I could somehow come up with a solution myself, but I have failed miserably. I'm now at breaking point; I need some guidance, and I need it NOW! After a lot of deliberation, I have finally decided that Linda is the only one who could help me sort out this mess. I'm positive she will be fair in her judgment. I can't wait any longer I need to speak to her tonight. John plays darts on a Monday so it will be a perfect opportunity to talk to her alone.

" How wis the honeymoon, MRS.? "   I asked giving her a big hug as she opened the door.

" It wis GREAT! What a difference it makes to hev the sun every day, and the Maltese people are so friendly. But I Wis so sorry to hear about your ma I wanted to be with you, " Linda said hugging me tight.

" Don't worry aboot it, ah know ye would hev been there if it hudnae been fir yer honeymoon. "

Linda looked relaxed, and full of the joys of being a new wife. I felt a bit guilty at interrupting her happiness with my problems, but I had no one else to turn to. I was desperate.

" You look great, we yer Malta tan. "

" Thanks, but how are you coping? " She said softly.

" I'm doing okay. "

" Whit aboot yer da. "

" Ah dinnae see much o' him. He goes tae the pub every night, and its better that way. Ah can suit ma sell, " I said as I opened my handbag.

I couldn't make any more small talk my pulse was racing, and I had to tell Linda now, before my head shattered into smithereens. I took the letters out of my bag, and threw them onto the coffee table. Looking at the pile of letters, I couldn't help feeling sad at never receiving any of them.

" Whits THAT? " Linda asked looking a bit startled.

" It's ma letters tae STEVE, and STEVE'S letters tae me"
I said trying to contain all my anger, and hurt as the memory of seeing those unopened letters for the first time flew back to me.

" WHIT! STEVE'S LETTERS! BUT! BUT! H O W! Where did they come fae? " Linda obviously shocked picked up the letters slowly realizing what this meant.

" Mum never posted my letters, and she kept Steve's letters hidden from me, " I revealed.

" OH! MY! GOD! How could she be so cruel? I can't believe she would do this to YOU! " Linda suddenly recognizing the severity of what these letters represented, and sat down beside me on the couch.

" I know, its hard tae absorb, but I found them in a little black box that mum kept locked away, " I blurted the words out quickly before my brain became dysfunctional.

I was now overwhelmed by the whole sad story; my emotions were ready to explode. I couldn't contain my feelings any longer. I broke down weeping with my face in my hands. Linda put her arm around me she didn't say anything she just held me tightly in her arms, and waited patiently allowing me to cry myself out, and hopefully release some of the tension inside my mind. Slowly I regained my composure.

" I don't know whit to say Patsy, I wish I could take away your pain. It must hev been horrendous finding oot that your mother had lied tae ye for aw these years, knowing how much you loved Steve, " Linda said softly now holding my hands.

" There's sumthing else, " I hesitated, I now felt a little guilty at not telling Linda before that I had seen Steve at the hospital.

" Good GOD! Patsy, Yer scaring me, " Linda looked extremely worried now.

" Ah never told ye this, but Steve wis the doctor looking after mum in the hospital. "

" WHIT! Ah don't BELIEVE IT! Patsy, " Linda was obviously dumbfounded with the news, and even more shocked that I had actually been in contact with Steve, and had never told her.

" A'm sorry, but ah never told ye because ye didnae need any o' ma troubles when ye were aboot tae get merried, " I said hoping Linda would understand my reasoning.

" Ah'm in complete shock, ah don't know whit tae say, "

Linda's eyes were opened wide like a detective scrutinizing the scene, trying to make sense of the evidence. She kept picking up the letters then putting them back onto the table looking for some clue to solve the predicament.

" I know whit yer going through it took ME a long time tae comprehend whit ma had done, but ma problem now is where do I go fae here? "

" Whit a bombshell Patsy, first ye tell me yer ma kept yer letters, then ye tell me ye'v seen Steve, and ye kept aw this tae yer sell...A'm a bit disappointed that ye never let me know sooner. Ye hev tae gee me time tae digest this, " Linda sat with a puzzled look on her face obviously unsure of what to say next.

" I know it's not easy to think that mum could cause me so much pain, but she did say that she was sorry when she was in hospital, and she did try to confess before she died. "

" SORRY! SORRY! Big deal. SHE'S SORRY! So she should be sorry after all the heartache she has caused ye, I don't know why yer no BITTER! Patsy. "

" Linda, I was devastated when I found the letters, I cried for days, and I thought I would hate her for the rest of my life, but when I eventually calmed down and considered her intentions, ah'm convinced she thought she wis doing it fir the best," I said, although I wasn't completely confident in my mind that was how I really felt, but it did help me to let go the pain.

" Naw! Naw! Yer wrang She's twisted, " Linda protested her anger evident, as she struggled to contain her emotions.

" Aw right then, but never mind HER ma MAIN problem is dae ye think ah should tell Steve, or jist forget it, and leave it in the past? " I said, raising my voice forcing Linda to let go of her anger towards my mum, and concentrate on Steve.

" It aw depends on how ye feel aboot Steve now? " She said letting her anger slowly recede.

" Aye, ah know! Linda, Oh! GOD! I'm ashamed tae say it. BUT! When ah saw him in the hospital standing at the side o' mum's bed, my heart done a back flip, I realised I hev never stopped loving him, I wanted to feel his arms around me forever. " It wasn't easy to be so honest not even with my best pal, but I knew I had to be true to myself, and Linda.

" Well then, that's yer answer, Patsy, ye know, ye only get one life, and if ye think that Steve is the love o' yer life then ye need tae tell him the truth. "

" BUT! Whit aboot ma Frankie? I don't want tae hurt him. I do love him, but in a different way, I didn't want to cause Frankie any pain. He has been so good to me, and I know how much he loves me. "I couldn't hold back the tears.

" Would ye want tae be second best Patsy? " Linda said putting her arm around me, and giving me another hanky.

" No, " I was now sobbing again on Linda's shoulder.

" Then DON'T make Frankie! That would hurt him even more, " Linda said softly, and I could hear the concern in her voice.

" Ye know, yer always right. Dae ye no get fed up being right aw the time? "

" NOT! REALLY! " She very quickly answered louder, and sharper than was necessary. We both laughed at Linda's abrupt reply. Allowing some of my sorrow to drift away.

Linda's advise was exactly what I felt subconsciously, but couldn't admit to my brain, but hearing those words has forced me into realising that I was only trying to deceive myself. Linda, I'm certain has helped me with one of the most difficult decisions I will ever have to make in my life. Linda's reaction I guess was exactly what I expected, but I still had to hear her say the words for me to convince myself that I was doing the right thing. Having Linda on my side wouldn't make the task of breaking up with Frankie any easier. But, she has helped to influence my decision, and I now know that I want to contact Steve, and explain to him the whole miserable tale.

But there's always the possibility that Steve might not be interested in me now. He probably hates me. He could, perhaps have a girlfriend back home in Halifax waiting for him.

But I still need to take the chance just in case he isn't involved with anyone, and he could maybe have some tiny feelings locked away just for ME!

Finding out how Steve feels about me now, means confronting him, and revealing all the evidence. I'm hoping with all my heart that in time he could be willing to forgive ME for giving up on him so easily, and my mum for her wrong doing.

BUT! There was something extremely important that I have to do first...

CHAPTER 46

The Promise

I was standing at the nurse's station, and I reluctantly watched as Patsy left the ward after her mother had died. She looked absolutely distraught with a brother on either side, supporting her body, and almost carrying her down the corridor. I desperately wanted to reach out, and hold her, but that wouldn't have been the right thing to do. I have to let her go.

It was only two days before Mrs. Stewart died that I learned the truth; Patsy's mum must have gone through agony before she confessed. Initially I was extremely angry with Patsy's mum. I just couldn't understand Why! She could do such a destructive thing to her only daughter?

And even after all these weeks I am still struggling to come to terms with Mrs. Stewart's confession. I can't help feeling I've been cheated out of a period in my life, that I should have spent with Patsy. My mind is in a complete turmoil not knowing if Patsy still has some love left in her heart for me.

Now after a considerable amount of deliberation, I am now more annoyed at myself than at Patsy's mum for not being more of a dominant character. I should have made more of an effort to find out all the facts before giving up completely on Patsy. I was a FOOL! I gave in far too easily.

I did, however promise Mrs. Stewart that I would tell Patsy the truth after she died. And I have spent hours and endless sleepless nights considering whether that was the right thing to do.

Finally I have decided that I have no option but to fulfil my promise. I feel it's only fair that Patsy is told the whole story, and given the opportunity to decide if she wants me in her life. I am now certain that I have never ever stopped loving Patsy. And I frantically need to know if she feels the same.

NOW! All I want to do is to talk to Patsy, and explain to her that I never stopped writing, and I never ever stopped loving her.

I have deliberately left contacting Patsy to give her time to come to terms with her mother's death. I have engrossed myself into my work diverting any temptation to pick up the phone to speak to Patsy, before she has had the time to grieve properly.

I still had Patsy's old phone number, and I'm hoping it hasn't been changed. As I dialled her number, I went from being a confident doctor, to a blundering ass, in a matter of seconds. I was so nervous I almost put the receiver down. I hope her dad doesn't answer the phone I can still remember him shouting at Patsy all these years ago. Then I heard Patsy's sweet voice.

" Hello, " Patsy said.

" It's Steve " a lengthy silence...

" Oh, Oh! " She whispered.

" PLEASE! PLEASE! Don't hang up; I need to talk to you, " I waited a second before continuing.

" Could you PLEASE? Meet me tonight I have something important to discuss with you please, " I pleaded before she had a chance to put down the receiver. Another big pause...for a second I thought she had hung up the phone.

" Emm, emm! Okay where? "

" It's a nice night; I thought we could take a walk around the park. "

" All right Steve, I'll meet ye in an hour, " I managed to say completely surprised, and intrigued by his call.

But, why did Steve want to talk to me? When he believes that I am a contriving bitch, who has treated him so badly, by not answering any of his letters. What could he possibly want to say to me?

CHAPTER 47

Meeting Steve

I saw Steve in the distance standing at the park gates. I had dreamt of this moment so many times in the last few weeks. I wanted to run up to him, and feel his arms around my body. I wanted to engulf myself in his scent, and breathe his fragrance forever. Why had I condemned him? I should have known he would never have ignored my pleas.

I feel so guilty. I am still unable to believe that my own mother could be so cruel. She had no excuse, she was totally aware of how devastated I was when those letters stopped coming, and yet she purposely kept them hidden. How could SHE! What kind of a mother could sit back, and watch her only daughter suffer so much hurt, knowing that she was the one inflicting the pain. It's beyond any understanding.

I am now only a few feet away from Steve and I could feel his eyes watching me closely as I got nearer to him. I saw his beautiful brown eyes, but this time I was looking at his eyes with love. Savouring every detail of his face.

And I am finding it extremely difficult to curb the urge I have kept buried inside of me for such a LONG! Long! Time. I want to be close to him, I want to feel his lips on mine once more.

Oh! GOD! I could hear my heart pounding inside my chest boom! Boom! Boom! My blood is unable to match the speed of my pulse. And, I could feel my body sway desperately struggling to compensate for my increased heart rate. Then everything went BLANK!

I saw Patsy approaching, walking slowly towards me. As she came closer I noticed, that she suddenly looked very pale, and unsteady on her feet. I saw her legs shake, and her body began to fall towards the ground. I quickly ran up to her, and caught her just before she fell to the ground.

I awoke to find Steve kneeling over me. He had carried me into the park, and laid me down on a bench. He was mopping my brow with water from the fountain. We looked into each other's eyes, transfixed in a capsule, and locking out the rest of the world. Transported back in time to 1970. Not wanting to THINK about anything.

He kissed me, and I kissed him back. I was in heaven. OH! GOD! Another magic moment to torture my SOUL!

" Hi there, you're a lucky lady there was a doctor around," He said staring into my eyes, and smiling.

" Yeah! Very lucky! " I said as I tried to sit up. But feeling shaken not by the fall, no it was the kiss that really affected me.

" How do you feel? " Steve asked obviously concerned.

" I'm fine, " I lied, now managing to sit up.

Steve sat down beside me, and I could see the tension tightening the muscles in his face making him appear solemn. And the atmosphere changed instantly, and he became very serious as he began to speak.

" Patsy, there's something I have to tell you, " the tone of his voice sounding very severe I wanted to stop the words coming out of his mouth.

" I don't want to know, lets just let it go, " I said very quickly not wanting to hear what he had to say.

" But, you don't understand, " he said gently taking hold of my hands.

" We can't go back Steve, " I said pleading with him to stop talking.

" But, it wasn't our fault, someone interfered with our love, " he said now extremely eager to tell me his news.

" How do you know THAT? " I asked shocked that he already knew. How could he know what mum had done?

" I'm sorry to be the one to tell you this, Patsy, but your mum confessed to me while she was in hospital, only two days before she died. And she made me promise that I would tell you once she had passed away. Patsy, your mum told me that she was deeply sorry, and she was very upset when she confessed believe me. It was the day you came into her room when she was howling and holding on to me. Do you remember? "

" Yes, yes but. "

" You see Patsy we weren't to blame, your mum had kept all my letters hidden from you, and she never posted any of your letters. " Steve explained anxious to inform me about the terrible deed mum had committed.

" Did she say WHY? She did it, DID She? " I was hoping, and praying that she had a genuine reason for her actions. Please god, let there be a very good explanation to justify what she had DONE!!! Let there be a saving grace, PLEASE!

" NO… But… You already know; don't YOU? " Steve said, now intrigued by my answer, and now slowly letting go of my hands.

" Yes, BUT! I only just found the letters the other day when I was sorting out all her bits, and pieces. And " I said, but had to stop to catch a breath of air.

" AND! And…. " Steve was impatiently waiting on a reply.

" I…decided it would cause ye too much hurt to reveal the truth, and I did'nae want to hurt you all over again. I have a good life with Frankie now, I'm really sorry Steve " I had to lie.

But her words were not what I expected to hear, causing me unbelievable PAIN! Patsy's greeny blue eyes fixed onto mine for a brief moment speaking a different language to what was coming out of her mouth.

" I see, I see, " I was in shock I had somehow managed to convince myself that we could start again, and I never considered a rejection. What a fool, I am.

Suddenly everything changed with those few words " I have a good life with Frankie ". It was not what I anticipated or imagined. I thought Patsy would fall into my arms, and we would be back on our bench in Filey again, and we would reminisce about all the good times, and perhaps end up singing " Hey Jude " all over again.
But instead I felt I had been kicked in the gut, and I wanted to be physically sick.
Patsy had moved on, she didn't feel the same. I had somehow forgotten to consider that she might not love me anymore. I didn't even get the chance to tell her that I never STOPPED Loving her.
I quickly collected my composure, and pretended not to be affected by her rejection. But in reality I was in delayed shock. I knew I would be in trouble later, when the full force of this refusal had hit me.

" W e l l, I'll walk you home if you like? " I said my voice sounding a touch high, but I was finding it difficult to talk my throat had suddenly lost all its moisture, and dried up.

" That would be fine. "

We left the park behind, and I managed (but I don't know how) to make general chit chat as we walked on our last journey together, but I couldn't trust myself to look into her eyes again.

We were now standing outside her home, I was kicking the dust on the ground with my shoes, and Patsy was staring into space obviously bored with my company. Neither of us said a word. And the silent was unbearable for what seemed like an eternity. But, although it was extremely uncomfortable being in her company I still wanted to be there and to stay close to Patsy for as long as I could.

But, I had to say goodbye, I had to be brave, I had to let her go.

" Well, I hope you have a happy life, " I really did want Patsy to be happy.

" Thanks Steve, you too, " I used all my strength to utter the words without breaking down.

We automatically gave each other a hug. And I wanted to hold on to her forever; but I couldn't hold on to a love that didn't feel the same. I had to release her. I wish now with all my heart that Patsy's mum had never confessed. If she had kept her secret quiet I wouldn't have to go through the pain of losing Patsy all over AGAIN!

I had built my hopes up far too high, and I never expected for a second that Patsy would turn me away. My heart has been crushed. AGAIN!

I silently stood, and watched as Patsy walked away hoping with all my heart that she might change her mind, and come running back down the stairs, and into my life once more. But she kept on walking, she never looked back.

Oh God! What do I do now?

Steve's scent is exactly the same as I remember. Oh, how I wish I could inhale his aroma for the rest of my life. But it was not to be! If only I had known sooner about the letters! Oh WHY! Oh Why! Hadn't I post them myself?

I walked away tears silently pouring down my face! I couldn't look back. Steve would know that I still loved him, if he saw my tormented eyes. I hauled myself up the stairs one by one using the banister as a guide to help me hoist my reluctant body away from Steve. Tears blinding my vision with each step taking me further, and further away from the man I love, but could NEVER have.

My heart is now screaming inside, my head pleading with me to STOP! STOP! Begging me to turn around, and run down the stairs into the arms of the man I have always, always loved.

I was now at the top of the landing, deeply concentrating on putting one foot in front of the other, forcing my legs to walk towards the door. I fumbled with my keys, and eventually I managed to open the front door.

I closed the door, and leaned all my weight heavily against the wall sliding slowly down to the floor. Sitting in a trance unable to move wishing my life could be different.

There was a lump stuck in my throat drying up my mouth, I'm positive my airway was now blocked stopping all the oxygen penetrating into my veins, I could hardly breathe the hurt was excruciating.

My breathing was now in short spurts. I desperately wished that the pain would disappear, and let me breathe. But my wound was somehow trapped inside my body, I couldn't reach it, and there was no way to escape the torture. The agony was unbearable.

Tears were gushing down my face, as I held my heavy head in my hands in a weak attempt to hide away from the world.

" Patsy is that you? " Dad shouted from the kitchen. His words startled me back to reality.

OH! NO! NO! PLEASE! OH! PLEASE! GOD! Don't let him come out of the kitchen I couldn't bear for him to see me in such a dreadful state.

" Aye dad it's me. " I used my last ounce of strength to shout the words. Praying it would be enough for him to stay away...

It was.

I sat on the floor slowly regaining my senses and reflecting on the last hour spent with my Steve.

Oh! GOD! WHAT! Had I done? Why did I let him go? Why did I pretend that I didn't care? Oh! God! When did my life become so crazy? I was distraught I wanted to quickly RUN!
YES! Back down those stairs two at a time, and tell him the truth. Kiss his sweet lips again, and again.
But I CAN'T!! I can't. I couldn't reveal my true feelings. It wouldn't be fair to Steve, or Frankie.
I will have to somehow forget my Steve, and perhaps, eventually one day the pain will go away.

My heart is dying, and resuscitation is not an option. How will I ever be able to function with a dead heart?

I now realize to my great sorrow that I could never love anyone the way I love Steve, but I have no OPTION! I have no CHOICE!!! I have to let him GO!

OH! GOD! I can't believe it, but Mum has controlled my destiny once AGAIN!

I'm going to have Frankie's baby...

Song References

" STAND BY ME "	Ben E. King
" SHE LOVES YOU "	Beatles
" SHOUT "	Lulu
" LONG AND WINDING ROAD "	Beatles
" ALL RIGHT NOW "	Free
" WILL YOU LOVE ME TOMORROW "	Carole King
" CRAZY "	Patsy Cline
" HEY JUDE "	Beatles
" SUNNY AFTERNOON "	Kinks
" DANCING IN THE STREET "	Martha And TheVandellas
" MY GUY "	Mary Wells
'YOU'RE MY WORLD "	Cilla
" YOU KEEP ME HANGING ON "	Supremes
" YESTERDAY "	Beatles
" IT'S OVER "	Roy Orbison
" IT'S NOW OR NEVER "	Elvis
" THE WONDER OF YOU"	Elvis

E.M. Shannon, her very first novel, spent her early years living in Glasgow. Now happily married for the second time, has 3 daughters and two step-daughters.

Made in the USA
Charleston, SC
12 June 2012